"*N*ick, it's only for the summer."

"You don't even act like you're going to miss me."

"Of course I'm going to miss you."

I was already missing him. It was like he'd gone away from the moment I'd first told him about my summer plans.

Maybe that's the reason I was now sitting on the shores of Lake Erie feeling lonely. We hadn't kissed good-bye. We'd barely *said* good-bye.

This was supposed to be a fun, exciting excursion. I didn't want to feel guilty about being here.

Bad news. I did.

Thrill Ride

RACHEL HAWTHORNE

AVON BOOKS
An Imprint of HarperCollins *Publishers*

Library of Congress Catalog Card Number:
2005906565
ISBN-10: 0-06-083954-6
ISBN-13: 978-0-06-083954-3

Typography by Karin Paprocki

First Avon edition, 2006

In memory of Fargo,
who always kept me company when I wrote.
We'll meet again at the rainbow bridge.

Chapter 1

Summer job possibilities . . . decisions, decisions

Work at Hart's Diner

Pros: Weekly paycheck; Nick, my new boyfriend, works there; chance to kiss in the cooler in between serving customers?

Cons: Aching feet; aching jaw from continually smiling to get better tips; living at home while Mom and older sister, Sarah, go through the insanity of planning Sarah's summer wedding (They can't agree on anything! Mom? Hello?!? Sarah is twenty-three, old enough to plan her own wedding. Note to self: Stay out of it!)

Work at the local movie theater

Pros: Weekly paycheck; watch the latest block-busters for free; eat complimentary no-limit-on-the-butter popcorn until I pop.

Cons: Aching feet from standing behind the concession counter; sweeping up spilled popcorn; sticky floors; see less of Nick; live at home while Mom and Sarah . . .

Work at amusement park near lake far, far away

Pros: Weekly paycheck; get on all the rides for free; gone all summer; dorms are available; being totally absent from home while Mom and Sarah . . .

Cons: Share a dorm room with someone I've never met; _never_ seeing Nick; and okay, I have roller coaster issues . . . like, I totally don't get what is so great about the whole queasy-stomach, heart-in-throat, up-and-down, faster, faster, higher, higher experience.

Decision: No brainer. Living with a stranger has got to be better than living with Mom and Sarah *while The Wedding is being planned. I don't have to ride the big roller coasters. It's only three months. True love can survive that, can't it?*

And that's how I, Megan Holloway, a life-in-the-slow-lane, carousel-ride type of girl, packed up the essentials of my life following my junior year in high school and headed to the Thrill Ride! Amusement Park, vacation destination extraordinaire on Lake Erie.

That afternoon I'd flown into the airport. With my backpack dangling off one shoulder, I pulled my large wheeled suitcase to the passenger pickup area outside the main terminal. An impossible-to-miss bright red Thrill Ride! shuttle bus was parked nearby, motor running.

So I headed over to it and peered in the door.

"Going my way?" I asked the driver.

He wasn't exactly what I was expecting. White-haired, wrinkled, slightly hunched. Still, he laughed and climbed out of the bus. "You here for the summer?" he asked.

"Yep."

He wore a red shirt, cargo shorts, and his name tag read PETE (SANTA FE, NM).

"You from Santa Fe?" I asked.

"Before I retired. Got tired of playing golf so came up here to work. Being around young people keeps me young."

He took my suitcase and put it in a holding bay at the back of the bus. "Climb aboard," he said.

I settled onto a seat. I heard laughter and two other girls clambered onto the bus.

"Hi!" one said.

"Hiya!" the other chirped.

"Hi." Not exactly an original response, and maybe part of the reason that our conversation didn't last longer.

They sat in front of me and immediately started talking to each other like long-lost friends. Pete returned to the driver's seat, closed the bus door, and headed away from the airport.

I figured the two girls were returning summer employees. Maybe a little older than me. Definitely friends. They were giggling, talking, and screeching periodically.

I looked out the window, trying really hard not to feel ignored and lonely. I *so* did not want to be lonely.

I was already missing Nick. We'd only been dating for three months, and he was totally bummed that I'd applied for a job at the park, and even more bummed that I'd been hired to work there for the entire summer.

"That sucks," he'd said.

Not exactly what I'd wanted to hear when I told him. I wanted him to be ecstatic about my good fortune. I mean, a thousand people had probably applied. I'd had to fill out an extensive application and submit an essay about the reasons that I wanted to work there. And I'd gotten in just under the wire on the minimum age requirement of seventeen. My birthday was yesterday.

So I'd been feeling pretty good about myself when I received the letter telling me that I'd been hired.

After I'd shared my good news with Nick, he'd moped around most of the evening. I'd shown him a video of the amusement park that my dad had ordered for me. My dad is really into watching the Travel Channel, so he was the one who discovered Thrill Ride! and told me about it. It sounded like it would be an awesome experience.

But Nick was less than impressed with the rides, the park, and all the facilities that the tour guide on the video walked us through. The video was geared toward enticing teens to come work there and making parents feel comfortable sending their kids off into the scary unknown. There were dorm moms and curfews and all kinds of safety features.

"It's just the same as Six Flags," he'd said. "You could have worked there over the summer, commuted from home, and been a lot closer to me."

"It's not the same. It's the thrill ride capital of the world. It's in another state. I want to live away from home. I'll be more independent. On my own. Or pretty much on my own. I mean, I'll live in a park-sponsored dorm, but gosh, Nick, no parents."

I'd tried to talk Nick into applying, so we'd

be together, but since he worked at Hart's Diner during the school year, he didn't feel like he could leave for the summer and expect to have a job when he got back. I admired his dedication, and totally understood his reasoning, even if I was a little hurt because it showed lack of dedication to our love.

But I didn't say anything to him about it, because I figured he could argue that my not hanging around showed *my* lack of dedication to our relationship. And while it would be a valid point, since he didn't live in my house, he had only an inkling of how insane it had gotten around there.

So I let the whole dedication-to-our-relationship thing slide.

Besides, I'd be gone only three months, and I was certain our love could sustain a short separation. People did it all the time.

All these thoughts were going through my mind as the shuttle bus took us out of the city and down a lonely road that seemed to lead into the heart of nothingness. But then the theme park became visible—or at least its tallest rides did. The roller coasters and vertical drops and

Ferris wheel. Why anyone would want to go up that high was beyond me. It made me dizzy just to think about it.

Beyond all the rides, I could see the lake. The park compound included all the rides, a huge hotel, and bungalows nearby. At the far edge, back a little way from all the tourist accommodations, was the employee dormitory.

The driver pulled to a stop in front of the large brick building. Compared to the hotel it was downright plain, but I didn't care. I didn't plan to spend that much time there, anyway.

I slung my backpack over my shoulder and disembarked. The two girls followed me off the bus, but then they released an ear-splitting squeal and were loping toward two other girls. More friends from summers past, I guessed. Great. I hoped I wasn't going to be the only one who didn't know anyone here.

I walked around to the back of the shuttle and took my suitcase from the driver. "Thanks," I said.

"Have a great summer," he said, with a smile and a wink. He reminded me a little of my granddad.

"I plan to," I assured him.

I pulled my suitcase along behind me as I headed to the dormitory. I went through the sliding glass doors and saw registration to my right.

I swallowed hard, the excitement mounting. I walked up to the desk and smiled at the girl behind it. Her name tag read MARY (BALTIMORE, MD). They hired students from all over the country, and I figured they felt like where you were from was as important as who you were.

"Welcome," she said, smiling brightly. "Are you here to check in?"

"Yeah," I said. I sounded a little breathless, part of my excitement and nervousness, not knowing what to expect, hoping everything was going to be okay. "I'm Megan Holloway."

She turned to a computer and began typing. Stopped. "Megan Holloway of Dallas, Texas?"

"That's me."

She searched through a drawer, pulled out a blue folder, and handed it to me. "You're assigned to room 654. Orientation begins at eight thirty in the morning. Don't be late.

You'll get your picture taken for your employee pass at that time." She winked at me. "I like to warn people because my first year here, I didn't know and I hadn't put on makeup. No retakes on the pictures. Not my best moment."

"I appreciate the warning," I told her, even if I wasn't heavy into makeup. Living in Texas blessed me with a permanent tan, so mascara and a touch of lip gloss were about all I ever used.

"Breakfast starts at six thirty," Mary continued. "A layout of the dorm is in your packet." She reached into another drawer. "And here's your name tag and a key to your room."

She placed a sheet of paper on the counter. "I just need you to sign that you received them."

My hand was actually shaking as I picked up the pen and signed my name. Everything was happening so fast. I couldn't wait to get to my room and calmly look through everything. Get oriented. Of course, I guess that's what morning orientation was for.

Mary took the sheet from me and dropped it into a wire basket where a stack of pages was already waiting. She gave me another one of her dazzling smiles. "Elevators are down that hallway to your right."

"Thanks."

"If you have any questions, there's an advisor on your floor. First door on your right."

On my right, on my right, on my right. Easy to remember. I had about a thousand questions, but I didn't even know where to begin, so I just nodded. "Thanks, again."

"Anytime." She looked past me. "Next?"

Oh, gosh, I hadn't realized that people were forming a line behind me. I moved away from the desk, giving the four girls and two guys an apologetic smile. I wondered if any were my roommate. Only one of them looked as nervous and apprehensive as I was.

I pulled my suitcase behind me, heading for the elevators. Off to my left, through double doors and plate glass windows, I could see the dormitory cafeteria. That was one of the neat things about working here: a room and food were provided at bargain-basement prices. I would have very little in the way of expenses, so I could save most of my paychecks through the summer and have money to get me through my senior year. I wouldn't have to work my last year of high school and could just enjoy the final months before I graduated.

I got to the elevators and pressed the button, my excitement mounting. And my apprehension. I could have requested a specific person to be my roommate—the only problem was, I didn't know anyone else who was working here.

I thought of getting to know a complete stranger as an adventure. It would be fun. I was sure of it.

The elevator arrived and took me up to the sixth floor. It didn't look that different from any of the hotels I'd ever stayed at. A long narrow hallway, doors on each side. Just as Mary (Baltimore, MD) had told me, the first door on my right had a sign:

FLOOR ADVISOR

ZOE (LONDON, ENGLAND)

How cool was that? I hadn't realized that the theme park was international, but why not? My excitement ratcheted up a notch. I thought about knocking on the door, introducing myself, but I was anxious to get to my room, see what it looked like, meet my roommate—if she was in.

At the end of the hallway I found room 654. Two pictures of Ferris wheels were taped to the door. On one was written MEGAN (DALLAS, TX) and on the other was JORDAN (LOS ANGELES, CA).

I tried to picture what a Jordan might look like, but decided the best way to satisfy my curiosity was to meet her.

I started to knock, then realized it was my room, too. I didn't have to knock. Might as well begin the way that I planned to continue. At least, that was my mom's favorite motto, especially when it came to guys and relationships. Be up front, be honest, be yourself. Basically, be who you were supposed to be.

The problem was that sometimes I wasn't quite sure who I was supposed to be. I mean I know who I am, but I am still trying to define myself, especially as a girlfriend, because every now and then, I do feel a twinge of guilt that I'd chosen working at an amusement park over Nick.

"Don't be silly," Sarah had said. "You're young! You have to explore options. Plenty of time later to put him first." Which, in retrospect, seemed odd advice from someone who was about to make a permanent commitment to a guy.

I slipped the electronic key into the slot, watched the green light come on, turned the knob, opened the door, stared in disbelief . . .

And wondered what in the world I'd gotten myself into.

Chapter 2

*I*t was unmistakably obvious that Jordan had moved in already. It was equally obvious that she didn't realize we'd only be here for three months or that she was sharing a room with someone. I gingerly made my way through the quagmire of crap that she'd left in the room: discarded boxes, strewn clothes, inline skates, tennis racket—did she think we were on vacation here?

A single bed was on either side of the room. On the far wall, a desk—one for me, one for my roomie—sat on either side of the window that looked out over the lake. The blinds were raised and I had a spectacular view of the water.

My desk had a phone. Hers had a computer,

a television, and an iPod speaker setup. I assumed since the bed on the right was covered in clothes that Jordan had claimed that side of the room. The dresser beside it was cluttered, the accordion door of her closet half open.

Sitting on what I perceived to be my bed, my solitary suitcase and backpack on the floor beside me, I wondered if I should try to find Zoe (London, England) and ask for a room transfer. My roommate was a slob. Not that I was a neat freak or anything—I mean, my mom had to threaten me with withholding my allowance to get me to clean my room—but let's get real here.

At home, the entire room was my domain. Here, we were supposed to learn about living with someone new, giving and taking equally, sharing, respecting the other person's space.

Jordan had three-fourths of the space already.

My impression of her had formed: slob, inconsiderate, disaster—

The phone rang.

I knew it couldn't be for me. I hadn't given anyone the number yet. Besides, I had a cell phone in the front pocket of my backpack that anyone who knew me would use. I thought about letting the phone on the desk go unanswered, but it goes against my nature. There's just something about the ringing of the phone that calls to me to pick it up. Even when I know it isn't going to be for me. So I did what any self-respecting girl would do. I snatched up the receiver.

"Hello?"

"Hey! Is this Jordan's room?"

"No, this is her *roommate*." I don't know what possessed me to toss out a smart comment, but the guy laughed.

"Pretty funny! Is she there?"

"Nope."

"Can I leave a message?"

"Sure."

"Just tell her, 'Cole loves ya.' "

"Okay."

"Thanks."

He hung up. I reached down, grabbed my backpack, set it on my bed, and pulled out my decision-maker. Compared to modern technology, my decision-maker was pretty old-fashioned:

a spiral notebook where I list the pros and cons for any major decision, so that I always make wise and informed choices. It's kind of an obsession with me. Sarah is always telling me that I take it to the extreme, but I believe in looking at all the options.

I turned to the last page, jerked out a blank sheet of paper, and wrote, "Cole called." No way was I going to get into delivering really personal messages about love. I folded the paper in half and set it on the edge of her desk, tucking a corner beneath her iPod speakers.

Obviously, my roomie had a boyfriend. I wondered if he was here. I thought about how nice it was that he'd called her, and it made me miss Nick more.

Nick was the absolute best. We had so much in common—went to the same high school, excelled in the same subjects, had the same friends. One night we'd all gone to the movies together. As usual Nick was sitting beside me. And, I don't know. The movie wasn't that good. Okay, it was really pretty terrible. And Nick leaned over and said exactly what I was thinking: We'll never get these hundred and twenty minutes of our lives back. And when I turned to reply, his face was so close to mine . . .

I didn't remember moving toward him, or him moving toward me. But suddenly we were kissing, and we'd been an item ever since. And we were going to remain an item even though we would be far apart. Me, up north on a great lake. Him down south in Texas.

We had e-mail and instant messaging and text messaging and our cell phones—we could manage.

Couldn't we? Sure we could. No sweat.

I was reaching for my cell phone to call him when the phone on the desk rang again. I almost let it ring, but in the end, I didn't have the willpower to deny the siren's call.

"Hello."

Silence. Great.

"Helllloooo?" I repeated.

"Sorry. Are you Jordan's roommate?"

Okay, I was starting to hate my roomie now. Another guy? And this one . . . oh my gosh, he had a voice like Brad Pitt, Orlando Bloom, and Colin Farrell all rolled into one. It just sent a shiver of pleasure through me. Really strange. I never reacted that way to a guy's voice. Not even Nick's. But this one . . . deep, smooth, just a little —

"You still there?" he asked.

I was totally embarrassed. I swallowed, cleared my throat. "Sorry. I got distracted watching the boats on the lake."

Yeah, right, Megan. "Uh, yes, I'm her roommate. She's not here. Did you want to leave a message?"

Even though my roommate was obviously an inconsiderate jerk, I wasn't going to stoop to that level. Sarah would be proud of me. She was always advising me not to get caught up in pettiness. Although I'd learned long ago that what she usually meant was, *don't argue with me.*

"Has anyone ever told you that you have an incredibly sexy voice?"

I held the phone away from my ear and stared at it. Had he said what I thought he had? First of all, my voice is not sexy. It's kind of raspy-sounding. Nick told me once that I sounded like his Aunt Carolyn who smoked cigarettes. Hardly flattering.

I knew this guy must be a major player. He was coming on to me and he didn't even know me. What a creep! The fact that I was thinking the same thing about his voice only seconds earlier didn't lessen my irritation with him. What kind of guy calls for one girl and flirts with another?

Jerk!

"Do you want to leave a message?" I asked, impatiently.

"What's your name?"

"My name?"

"Yeah. I bet it's as intriguing as your voice."

"Hardly."

"Let me be the judge. What is it?"

"Is that the message you want to leave for Jordan? That you want to be a judge?"

He laughed. Big mistake to make him laugh because the deep rumble shimmered down to my toes and made them curl. Laughter never made my toes react. This was too totally strange.

"Come on, what's the big secret? Is it something embarrassing maybe? Millicent?"

I rolled my eyes. "No."

"Bambi?"

I ground my teeth together. "No."

"Come on. There's no way it's as bad as my name."

"What's your name?" I asked.

"I thought you'd never ask. Parker."

I scowled. His name wasn't bad at all. Had he tricked me into expressing an interest in him?

"So I can tell her Parker called?"

"Who's going to tell her?"

I swear I heard him smile. I know that's impossible, but it sure sounded like a smile in his voice. I relented.

"Megan."

"I like it."

"My mom would be thrilled to know she has your seal of approval."

He laughed again. It was an infectious laugh. It made me want to laugh with him, but I was so not going to play his game.

"Look, I'm really busy here," I said.

"Watching the boats?"

"Unpacking."

"We could watch them together."

"Do you not listen? I'm unpacking."

"So you just got there?"

"Yeah."

"Met Jordan yet?"

"Not in person, no."

"But you see evidence of her personality?"

"Definitely."

"Let me guess. Clothes everywhere. Looks like a tornado ripped through the room."

"Sorta. Look, I really need to go."

"Gotcha. It was nice to meet you."

"We didn't actually meet."

"Close enough. Just tell Jordan I called."

"I will."

I hung up, grabbed the piece of paper with her previous message, scrawled another name, and set it back in place. I was obviously rooming with Miss Popularity.

Already, I regretted taking my chances with a roommate. Not that I really had any other choice. I didn't know anyone who was working at the amusement park, and even if I had managed to convince Nick to join me, the dorm policies prohibited girls and guys from sharing a room.

The questionnaire I'd completed requesting

a room had asked only one question regarding roommate preference: Do you smoke?

So all I really knew about Jordan was that she didn't smoke, and she was a slob, a guy magnet, and from Los Angeles. Not exactly resounding endorsements.

I walked to the window and looked out onto the lake. I could see the boats that I'd fibbed about watching: sailboats and speed boats. People were spread out on blankets and beach towels on the sand near the water, absorbing the last rays of the late May sun. The next weekend would kick off the summer and the theme park would go into high gear. Right now the park opened late in the morning and closed at seven in the evening. This week was training for the new employees.

The door suddenly sprang open. I whipped around.

And there was my roommate. Had to be. She was way shorter than me, maybe five-five to my five-nine. She had short, cropped hair the color of a midnight sky and sapphire blue eyes.

"Oh, gosh! I'm so sorry!" she exclaimed,

moving into the room like a strong wind was pushing her. "I'd planned to get back and get everything cleaned up, but then Ross wanted to go to the lake, and I couldn't find my bathing suit."

And who was Ross? Guy number three?

She dropped two large shopping bags on her bed. "Can you believe that I didn't pack my bathing suit? *Hello?!?* We're on a lake! How dumb was that? Totally. So we had to go to the mall, and wouldn't you know it? They were having a beginning of summer sale, and no way could I buy only a bikini. You know?" She hopped over a box and grinned at me like she'd won something. "I'm Jordan, by the way. In case you didn't figure that out." Her eyes got really big. "Which I'm sure you probably did. Because you look like you're really smart."

I just stared at her. I'd never had anyone talk nonstop for so long. Was she on some sort of drugs? And what did really smart look like?

She laughed. "You're Megan, right?"

"Right."

"Well, it'll only take me about fifteen minutes to get everything picked up." She jerked her thumb toward the door that led into the bathroom and whispered, "Our suitemates are total slobs."

Our room had a bathroom that connected to the room next door. I hadn't even thought to check it out, but I was also totally stunned that she'd think anyone was a slob. My mom told me once that people never see their own faults but will see them in other people. That was certainly true of my roomie.

Although she *had* spoken the truth about cleaning up quickly. It wasn't taking her long at all, mostly because she was just closing up boxes and stacking them in the closet, tossing clothes in drawers. She definitely took the minimalist view on tidy.

"So you're from Dallas, huh? We've been there a couple of times for vacation and stuff, mostly at the airport, passing through, you know? On our way to someplace else. Is this your first time working here?"

I was getting dizzy. "Yep."

She laughed. "Yep? That sounds so Texan. You don't have much of an accent. I thought Texans had slow drawls."

"Depends on which part of Texas you're from." I was anxious to get the conversation turned away from me. "By the way, you got some phone calls while you were out." I pointed at her desk.

"Oh, gosh, I didn't think anyone would ever call me here." Jordan snatched up the sheet of paper and scanned it. "Cole called! That was so sweet of him. Did he say anything special, why he called?"

I shrugged, shook my head. He could tell her when he saw her that he loved her. "Not really."

"Huh. He usually leaves a 'love ya' message, as his signature. I've never figured out why, but that's Cole. Lots of love. How about Parker?" Her voice softened with the mention of his name. "He didn't leave a message either?"

Again I shook my head.

"I'm surprised he called. He hates talking on the phone."

Could have fooled me. The guy was a regular chatterbox.

Jordan picked up the receiver and began

pressing numbers. She gave me a wink as she waited.

"Hi! I know! I know!" She bobbed her head from side to side. "I went shopping and I had my cell phone with me, but I'd forgotten to recharge it . . . I know, I know, I'll charge it tonight. Yeah, she seems really nice. So I was worrying for nothing. Just like you said. I'm going to come over later. Okay . . . See you in a bit. Love ya . . . Bye."

Jordan hung up. "Parker . . . he is just so cool. He's worked here two summers already so he knows everything and everyone. I'm going to have him give me some tips for tomorrow."

"Does he live in the dorm?"

"No way! He's nineteen, already had a year away at college, totally out on his own. No way would he live somewhere with a curfew. He's living in a little house on the lake down the way."

I understood why Jordan was a short person. Any energy her body would have needed to expend in growing had been used up talking. She didn't even stop to breathe.

A knock sounded on the door. She bounced

over and flung it open. A tall, slender guy with brown hair hanging past his ears was leaning against the doorway.

I could only hope that this wasn't guy number four.

Chapter 3

"I'm starved," he said. "We gonna eat or what?" The hint of irritation in his voice didn't match the sparkle in his brown eyes.

I wasn't surprised to see a guy in the doorway. I knew both guys and girls lived in the dorm. Some on the same floors, just not in the same rooms or suites.

Jordan pointed her fingers between us. "This is Ross. Ross, this is my roomie, Megan."

Ah, we were back to guy number three.

Ross gave me a warm smile. "Hi. Newbie?"

"Yeah."

"Me, too." Ross's gaze went back to Jordan. "I'm really hungry."

"Wanna come with us?" Jordan asked me.

"They don't serve dinner in the cafeteria on Sunday night."

Decisions . . . decisions . . .

Go to dinner with Jordan and Ross . . . or finish unpacking and call Nick. No-brainer. I really needed and wanted to talk with Nick.

"Thanks, but I need to take care of some stuff here."

"Okay, cool. We'll catch you later." She drew a circle with her finger. "I swear before we go to sleep that I'll have everything put away."

"Not a problem." A little lie, maybe, because I didn't want to spend the summer putting my life at risk in this obstacle course of a room. But I didn't want to start out as a difficult roommate, either.

She and Ross left, and I began putting away my few belongings. I didn't need that many clothes because I knew I'd have a uniform to wear while I was working. As for TV, stereo, etc., I had my own iPod—no speakers—and my laptop and that was about it.

My cell phone rang. With my luck, it would

be another boy calling Jordan. Ridiculous thought. So she had boys coming out the wazoo. Big deal. I took my phone out of my backpack, looked at the number, and smiled. My sister. I flipped it open. "Hey, Sarah!"

She groaned melodramatically. "Are you ready to come home?"

I laughed. "I just got unpacked. Too late now!"

"So what's it like?"

"I've been here only an hour, but first impressions? It's going to be totally cool." I didn't want to tell her my doubts about my roommate. Otherwise she'd start hounding me to come home. She was almost as thrilled as Nick about my coming here. According to her, I'd abandoned her in her hour of need.

"Mom is driving me absolutely crazy," she said.

"Why do you think I took this job way up here?"

"Chicken! Maybe I'll go up there and move in with you."

"Thought you were going to move in with Bobby."

"Yeah, but not until after we're married, and that's not for several more weeks—if I survive. The latest is that Mom thinks my wedding dress is too daring for church. You've seen it. What do you think?"

The neckline *was* low.

"Do you have to get married in church?"

"You agree with her?"

"The gown is pretty revealing. I mean, it wouldn't be on me, because I don't have that much to reveal, but you are an entirely different story." It was hard to believe we came from the same gene pool. We both had brown eyes but that was about where the similarity ended. I was tall, slender—okay, I'm being generous. I had to run around in the shower to get wet. I really got tired of hearing girls complaining about their excess weight, when no matter what I ate, I stayed thin. And hopelessly flat-chested. I had brown hair, highlighted, that was presently clipped to the back of my head. Sarah was a tad shorter, had blonde hair, highlighted, too, and she was one of the people who always complained to me about her weight, but of course she's gorgeous and has amazing curves. Gag, gag, gag.

"Why didn't you say something about the neckline when I was ordering it?" she asked now.

"Number one, you were looking in a three-way mirror, so I figured *you* could see that half your boobs were showing, and number two, because it's your wedding. You should wear what you want."

"You're doing your usual exaggeration thing, right? I mean, half my chest isn't exposed."

"Almost."

"Shoot. I hate for Mom to be right."

I smiled. That was part of the reason that so much yelling was going on at the house right now. Mom and Sarah are both stubborn, convinced that her way is the only way. For Sarah to even hint that Mom might be right was major.

"So what are you going to do?" I asked.

"Guess I'll see about changing out the gown, except that my one and only sister abandoned me for Canada—"

"I'm not in Canada."

"You might as well be. Just cross the lake and you're there."

"Do you have any idea how big Lake Erie is? It's like looking out on an ocean. You can't see the other shore."

"That's not the point. The point is, how can I go shopping for a gown without you to help me make a selection? You're my maid of honor."

"Take Lena with you."

Lena is her best friend and one of the six bridesmaids.

"I will, but I like having you there, too. Maybe you could fly home for the weekend."

I laughed. "Sarah, I had to sign a blood oath that I would ask for only one weekend off all summer. And I'm taking it to go to your wedding."

"That sucks. You being there sucks. I never thought I'd say this, but I miss you, Megan. What were you thinking when you took a job so far away?"

"I was thinking it would be a lot better than a summer of listening to you and Mom fight all the time."

"We don't fight. We just don't ever agree."

"You fight."

"Okay. We fight. I'll send you a picture of the new gown that I pick out and you can tell me what you think."

"Okay."

"Okay," she said, sadness in her voice. "What's it really like there?"

"I'm not sure yet. Ask me tomorrow."

"Okay. I gotta go. Love ya."

"You, too."

I hung up. I sometimes thought that the reason that Mom and Sarah fought so often was because they were so much alike. Headstrong, determined, bossy. I was more like Dad: laid-back, quiet, didn't let too much bother me. Which was the reason that I'd thought I wouldn't have much trouble adjusting to living with someone I didn't know.

And maybe Jordan wasn't that bad. I mean, she'd realized that she needed to pick up her mess and she'd done it . . . almost. It could work between us.

I went back to unpacking. Like I said. I didn't have that much. My clothes went into the closet or in the dresser beside my bed. My toiletries went into the bathroom. I didn't think our suitemates were slobs, but four girls, two sinks, and one counter did make for a lot of clutter. My laptop went on my desk where the DSL connection would keep me connected to the world. I put a few odds and ends on shelves nailed to the wall over my desk and placed my alarm clock on my desk next to the computer so it was near my bed for easy reach.

I looked at my watch. It was already seven. The sun was setting. I thought about calling Nick, but I guess I was being a little stubborn, hoping he'd call me.

This was insane. I grabbed my phone, slipped it into the pocket of my cargo shorts, along with my key, and headed out the door. A few people were in the hallway, and I sorta felt like I was walking a gauntlet.

"Hey!" girls said, as I passed.

The conversations were all the same. Name. Town. State. Laugh. First time? Yes. No. Just the facts, ma'am. And on I walked.

I got to the end of the hallway where the advisor's room was. A girl with spiked black hair was standing in the doorway.

"'Ello!" she said. "And who might you be?"

No doubt. She was Zoe (London, England).

"I'm Megan."

"Meg! It's great to meet you."

"Megan."

"Oh, a purist, eh? I'm Zoe." She pointed to the sign. "Floor advisor. Come to me if you have any problems, luv."

Her accent was delicious.

"I was going to take a walk by the lake."

"Brilliant! It's lovely out. Just don't forget about the curfew. One o'clock and we lock everything up."

I laughed. "No way will I be out until one."

"Don't be so sure; it gets addictive. Especially when a hottie catches your fancy."

She was probably only a couple of years older than I was. I thought I could have been content to spend all night talking with her, but I did want to take that walk, so I headed out.

Down the elevator, through the lobby, out the front door. I walked along the sidewalk that went around the building until it ended at the sand. I kicked off my sandals and walked toward the water. I touched the water's edge with the tips of my toes. It was freezing!

And Jordan had gone out to buy a bathing suit? My roomie was a crazy girl.

I sat down on the sand, drew my legs up to my chest, and wrapped my arms around my knees. I hadn't expected to be homesick after just one day. I was sorta wishing Sarah hadn't called. Who would have thought that I'd miss her squabbling with Mom?

I took my cell phone out of my pocket and willed it to ring. Now I was being as stubborn as my sister, but I guess the truth was, Nick had hurt my feelings a little bit. I mean, here I was going on an adventure, and he didn't want to share it with me.

Not the actual coming here. I really did get why he couldn't just pack up and leave his job. But when I'd gone shopping for the things I'd need, like new clothes, he had no interest in going with me. When I researched on the Internet to figure out how inconvenient it would be not to have a car, he didn't care about my findings. It was like Thrill Ride! or anything to do with it was totally off-limits, as far as a topic of conversation.

Surly. That's how he'd get. I'd read the word in novels, but had never actually seen anyone who was surly. Nick had been.

"This sucks big time," he'd said last night.

We were sitting in his car in my driveway. He'd taken me to dinner at Outback to celebrate my birthday.

"Let's not say good-bye tonight," I said. "Take me to the airport in the morning."

"Why? It's just putting off the inevitable."

"But it's more romantic at an airport."

"I don't see how. I wouldn't be able to go to the gate with you because of all the security stuff. We'd have to say good-bye outside the metal detectors. What's romantic about that?"

I'd sighed. "Well, then, I guess we'll say good-bye now."

"Yeah." He'd put his arm around me, drew me up against his side. "I'm sorry, Megan. It's just that I had plans for this summer, plans that included you and me, getting really close." He touched his forehead to mine. "You know?"

And I did know. He'd been pushing for us to take our relationship to the next level, but I wasn't ready yet. I mean I loved him, I was sure I did, but right now I was happy just kissing and snuggling.

I angled my face for easier access and kissed him. His arms tightened around me.

"God, I'm going to miss you, Megan. I don't know how I'll survive."

That's what a girl wanted to hear. Deep devotion. But it was only three months, and not all at once. I'd be back halfway through the summer for the wedding. And didn't absence make the heart grow fonder?

Then Nick was seriously kissing me, hard, our teeth clicking, like he thought he could save our kisses or something. I pulled back. "Nick! Don't be so . . . eager."

"Most girls would like to be wanted as much as I want you."

"But you were bruising my lips."

"Sorry. Do you have to go?"

"You know I do. I gave them my word."

And that's when he started to sulk. It suddenly got really cold in the car, a drop in temperature that had nothing to do with the air surrounding us, and it frightened me a little to think that I might lose him, but it also frightened me to think that I was making my decisions based on what was best for Nick, rather than what was best for me.

"Look, I'm not begging you to leave Hart's," I said. "I understand that you have a commitment there. Well, now I have a commitment."

"Thought you were committed to me."

I groaned. "Nick, it's only for the summer."

"You don't even act like you're going to miss me."

"Of course I'm going to miss you."

I was already missing him. It was like he'd gone away from the moment I'd first told him about my summer plans.

Maybe that's the reason I was now sitting on the shores of Lake Erie feeling lonely. We hadn't kissed good-bye. We'd barely *said* good-bye.

This was supposed to be a fun, exciting excursion. I didn't want to feel guilty about being here.

Bad news. I did.

Chapter 4

On the way back to my room, I stopped off at the vending machines and bought some peanut-butter crackers and a Mountain Dew, my favorite snack.

But my first night away from home, out on my own, and this was how I celebrate? Vending machine?

At least it was cheap, leaving me lots of money for another night. By the time I got to my room, it was almost nine o'clock. I didn't realize that I'd sat by the lake for so long. Jordan was back, the room was tidied up, but it was no less crowded. We had guests.

"Roomie!" Jordan exclaimed as soon as I walked in. "Meet our suitemates: Alisha, Washington, D.C., and Lisa, Toronto, Ontario.

Is it not totally cool that everyone is a name and a place? It's awesome to think of all the different people we'll meet. The places they'll come from. Totally wild experiences."

Alisha had short, black hair, dark eyes, and a milk-chocolate complexion. She was Halle Berry gorgeous. Lisa had curly red hair, an abundance of freckles, and an impish smile. Not to be mean, but she reminded me of a leprechaun.

"I was just telling them that they could use my fridge in the bathroom," Jordan said.

"You have a fridge?" I asked.

"Well, yeah! This is like dorm life, you know. Before I left home, Parker told me everything I'd need. I've got a microwave, too."

She patted the microwave sitting on her dresser. When had she moved in the appliances? I had a feeling that my roommate was going to be a constant source of surprises.

"We're all newbies," Jordan said. "None of us have ever worked here before."

"Which I think puts us on the take-what-you-get list as far as positions at the park goes," Alisha said.

"Hey, everyone, let's sit down, let's talk," Jordan said. She promptly dropped to the floor.

The dorm rooms had no chairs other than the straight-backed ones at the desks. Hardly comfortable. The rest of us sat on the rug with Jordan.

"Okay, so," she said with excitement, like someone who was in charge of a field trip, "what did everyone request as a job?"

"Rides," Lisa and I said at the same time. Then we smiled at each other. The choices were rides, concession, entertainment, mascot, gift shop.

"I put it in for mascot. Since I'm a cheerleader, I figured it was a natural spot for me," Jordan said. "What about you, Alisha?"

I was so not surprised to discover that Jordan was a cheerleader. Probably head cheerleader at that.

"Entertainment."

"Totally cool! What do you do?"

Alisha looked slightly embarrassed. "A little dancing, singing. I actually want to be an actress."

"Awesome!" Jordan said.

"You'll have to try out, won't you?" I asked.

"Yeah. I actually have an audition tomorrow afternoon after orientation."

"You'll get a spot on the stage," Jordan said, complete confidence in her voice.

"How do you know?" Alisha asked, not sounding quite as confident.

"Positive thinking. Works every time. It's all about the vibes you put out there. Just go in there tomorrow thinking, 'This spot is mine.' You'll get it guaranteed. I'm certain that I'm going to get to be Thumbelina."

Thrill Ride! had all kinds of fairy-tale characters in costume, wandering around throughout the park to entertain kids.

My stomach rumbled. The three girls looked at me, and I held up my crackers and drink. "Dinner."

"You're kidding," Jordan said. "You gave up dinner with me for that?"

I shrugged. "I ended up walking along the beach until it got dark. And since I don't have a car—"

"I do. Want me to take you somewhere?"

Jordan asked.

I was grateful for her offer, but it really seemed like an imposition. "No, but thanks. I'm fine tonight."

"The hotel actually has this little mini mall, food court area," Alisha said. "Lisa and I had pizza over there tonight."

"It was pretty good," Lisa said. "They're open until eleven."

"Then let's go!" Jordan said.

Alisha laughed. "You have way too much energy, girl."

"Really, guys, thanks," I interjected. "But y'all have eaten and I'm tired. Think I'm just going to have a few crackers, give my boyfriend a call—"

"You have a boyfriend?" Alisha asked.

I felt myself blushing. "Yeah."

"Does he work here?"

"No, he has a job back home, so he couldn't come."

"Bummer."

"Yeah."

Boy, was I a conversational genius tonight or what? I just couldn't seem to get over this bout of self-consciousness I was feeling, or maybe I was simply subconsciously really upset that Nick hadn't bothered to call.

No subconsciousness about it. I was bothered.

There was still a lot of excitement in the air as our suitemates said goodnight and exited through the bathroom into their room.

"Aren't they great?" Jordan asked, but it was more an exclamation than a real question.

"Yeah." There I was, Miss-Stuck-on-One-Word.

"This is going to be the absolute best summer ever," she said.

"Absolutely." Finally, I seemed to have moved beyond my stuck word.

"So what's your boyfriend like?" Jordan asked.

"He's wonderful, he's . . ." How to describe him?

"It must have been hard to leave him."

"Definitely." My vocabulary was increasing. I lifted my phone. "I'm going to call him now."

"Oh, sure! Sorry, didn't mean to keep you

from it. I'm going to get ready for bed." She gathered up her clothes and disappeared into the bathroom.

I sat on my bed and stared at my phone. We were in the same time zone. It was almost ten now. Not too late to call.

My phone rang and I nearly dropped it. My chest tightened with joy. Nick!

"Hello?"

"Hey, Megan."

"I was just about to call you."

"Really?" He sounded relieved, like maybe he was as insecure with how we'd left things last night as I was.

I settled back against my pillow, smiling. "Yeah."

"I'm sorry about last night. I'm not going to see you for almost two months, and I didn't even give you a proper kiss. I'm a total jerk."

My heart just melted. Nothing like an apology to make everything all right with the world.

"I could use a kiss right about now," I said.

He made smacking noises, and I started laughing. When he stopped, I said, "Thanks,

Nick. I needed to know you weren't still mad at me."

"I actually went to the airport this morning, to say good-bye."

"You did?" My heart was expanding.

"Yeah, but since we're not related, security wouldn't let me through to the gate."

"I'm sorry."

"No biggie. I'll be waiting at baggage claim when you get back for the wedding."

"Oh, Nick." I felt tears sting my eyes. I could turn into a puddle of emotion so easily. It really didn't take much.

"Don't suppose you'll come back tomorrow?" he asked.

"I can't, Nick."

"All right. Love ya, Megan."

"Love you, too."

He made a few more kissing sounds; so did I. Then we hung up. I held my cell phone close against my chest, like it would bring me nearer to Nick. It was going to be all right, being away from him for a while. People survived long-distance relationships all the time.

Jordan came out of the bathroom. "How'd it go?" she asked.

I smiled. "Good. He misses me."

"Sounds like a perfect boyfriend."

She would know. At last count, I think she had at least three. Or maybe they were just boys who were friends. It happened.

I changed into my sleeping boxers and tank and crawled into bed. Jordan turned off the light.

Then I just lay there in the dark, in a room that wasn't my bedroom with someone who I'd only met a few hours before. It was kinda strange, and I wondered if I'd even be able to sleep with a stranger in the room.

"Are you scared, Megan?" she asked, suddenly.

"Of what?"

"I don't know. Just being out on your own."

"Yeah, a little, but I figure next year after I graduate and go off to college I'll be on my own for real."

"You're a senior?"

"Yep."

"Me, too. So what made you decide to come here?" she asked.

"Honestly?"

"Yeah."

"My sister, Sarah, is getting married July fifteenth, and it was driving me crazy to be around while she and my mom planned the wedding."

"Really?" I heard a tinge of excitement in her voice. "Like what were they doing?"

"Well, for starters, Sarah wanted to be married in a park, Mom wanted her married indoors. Mom won, since in July it's hot beyond belief in Texas."

"That's what I've heard."

"Then they were arguing about how big to make the wedding party, what color the brides-maids' dresses should be—Sarah wanted black."

"What's wrong with black?"

"Mom says it's taboo for a wedding."

"I see people in black at weddings all the time."

"Apparently my mom hasn't. That one had

them yelling. Mom said she wasn't paying for a funeral. They argue about everything. They can't agree on the simplest of things. I'm definitely eloping."

"Me, too, I'm going to Vegas and getting married by Elvis."

I laughed. "Are you really?"

"Either that or never getting married."

"I don't know that I could take my marriage vows seriously if they were overseen by Elvis, but I definitely want small and away from home."

"They marry people here."

I stared into the darkness. "I didn't know that."

"Yeah. They have this little park with a bridge. It's kinda neat." She yawned. "Probably see it tomorrow when they take us on a tour of the place. Parker says he's getting married on a roller coaster. He is so crazy."

"Sounds like."

"This is his third summer here, so he's already working. He actually oversees Magnum Force. That's the tallest, fastest roller coaster. He has to ride it every morning before the park opens. I'm going to go ride it with him in the morning. Want to come?"

Ride Magnum Force? I don't think so.

"Uh, thanks, but we have orientation."

"We're going to ride at six, so we'll be back in plenty of time."

"I can't do rides on an empty stomach. Besides, I have some things I have to take care of in the morning."

"Okay. Whatever." She yawned again. "'Night."

"'Night."

I heard her bed creak as she rolled over. I should have been tired. It was late and I'd left home early that morning. But my mind was reeling with the possibilities. I really hoped that I didn't get assigned to one of the roller coasters. There were like fifteen or so. It had never occurred to me that I'd have to actually get on the ride where I worked.

Geez. That would be disastrous because I absolutely, no way, could get on a roller coaster.

Only 55 Nick-less days to go, and count-ing. . . .

Chapter 5

$\mathcal{A}$s it turned out, I could have slept without worries. As a matter of fact, I might have even welcomed riding a roller coaster.

I was assigned to the Hansel and Gretel gift shop, otherwise known as H & G, or as I was beginning to think of it: hell and god-awful. Because, of course, since this was a *theme* park — theme being the operative word here — I was scheduled to show up in wardrobe for sizing at two o'clock. And I didn't have to ask what my costume would be.

"At least the gift shop is air conditioned," Jordan said, swirling her French fry around in a glob of ketchup. "I mean, I'm going to be standing out in the hot sun all day saying, 'Please exit to your right. Watch your step.' Can you believe they gave me a script for this?"

They'd given everyone a script of things to say and not say. Rules and regulations to follow. We'd been given a mission statement, a purpose, and a rousing pep talk.

Then we'd walked through the entire park, while its history was revealed to us by a very energetic guy named Bill (Waterloo, Ontario).

The most fascinating of all the rides to me were the carousels: original pipe organs, original wooden horses—restored by artisans. They actually had three carousels in the park, and I wished that I'd been given one of them as my assignment. Those who took care of the rides wore cargo shorts, red shirts, white socks, tennis shoes, and red baseball caps. They could wear their hair however they wanted. Me? I was going to have to wear braids on each side of my head. I was seriously contemplating a major haircut.

Throughout the tour, Ross had stuck to Jordan like paper to glue, but not in an overtly romantic way. They realized that they were at work and not on a date, but still it made me miss Nick all the more to see them together.

The park was open but hardly crowded, since the "season" hadn't officially started.

When the tour was over, we broke for lunch. Now the three of us were sitting at a table in the food court area of the theme park.

"So what are we going to do this afternoon?" Ross asked.

"Wanna go sailing?" Jordan asked.

He grinned. "Sure."

Jordan looked at me. "Wanna come with us?"

"You have a boat?" I asked.

She laughed lightly. "No. Down the lake a ways they have rentals."

"I'd love to but I need to go to costume."

"Oh, right. Gretel. Wonder how long it'll take."

I shook my head. "No idea, but since everyone is getting fitted this afternoon"—I wrinkled my nose—"you probably shouldn't wait on me."

"Okay, but let me give you my cell phone number in case they cut you loose quickly. We can always come back for you."

That was so nice. As we exchanged numbers,

I was thinking that maybe things were going to work out with my new roomie after all.

I stood in front of the mirror in costume, fighting back my strong urge to yodel. My costume had a white blouse with short puffy sleeves, a short black skirt with a bib that came up the front and straps that went over the shoulders and crossed in the back, and a petticoat. Oh, yeah. And white knee socks and black shoes.

"The only thing that could be worse than this is to be Hansel," said Patti (Weed, CA). She was tall like me, but not as slender. Healthy, my grandmother would have called her.

I bit back my laughter. "I don't know. This is pretty bad."

"Do you think we got this gig because we have long hair? I mean, give me a break. Tomorrow we have to braid it." Her hair was long, blonde, and wavy.

"I'm thinking of buzzing mine tonight," I confessed.

She laughed. "I always thought of Gretel as being petite. We're both pretty tall."

"I think you're right—it's the hair."

"At least we'll be in air-conditioning."

"That's what my roommate says."

"What did she get assigned?" Patti asked.

"One of the kiddie coasters."

"Lucky girl."

Although I wasn't sure how lucky it really was. I mean, dealing with tired kids on a hot day? Ross would be working at Jet Scream, a ride that went straight up and spiraled down, and had a puke factor of ten. They even had a special cleanup crew for any "incident," as our tour guide had so politely referred to it.

Working inside a gingerbread-designed gift shop was sounding better all the time. And, at least, back home I would never run into anyone who saw me this summer, so the embarrassment factor was lowered.

After Patti and I changed back into our regular clothes, we took our costumes to a window. A middle-aged woman named Jeannie (no city, no state) was working behind it. She took our costumes, scanned the bar codes that were located on tags inside them, then swiped our park ID badges through the machine.

"All righty. You'll pick these up in the morning before work, change in the locker room, then drop them off after work so they can be washed for the next day," she said briskly.

"Wouldn't it be better if we took them with us and just washed them ourselves?" Patti asked.

"Weren't you paying attention during orientation, honey?" Jeannie asked. "Everything is computerized. I'll swipe your badge in the morning, and I'll know exactly where your costume is on the rack. Runs like clockwork."

"Sounds great," I said, not at all disappointed that I didn't have to wash clothes every night.

"What now?" Patti asked me as we turned away from the window.

"I don't know." I thought about joining Jordan for the sailboat ride, but I didn't feel like being a third wheel.

I ended up spending the afternoon lounging out by the pool. Nothing too exciting. I could hear the rumble of the roller coaster nearest the dorm. Magnum Force. It was a steel roller coaster, so it didn't have all that clacking noise, but still it sounded fast. And of course, I could hear people scream.

I just so didn't get that.

When I got back to the room, a note from Jordan was resting on my computer.

Dear Gretel:

Ha! Ha! Very funny, I thought.

Sorry we didn't connect.

I'm going to have dinner at Parker's.

Be back late! Don't wait up!

Your Roomie, Roller Coaster Gal

That was interesting. Dinner with Parker after spending the day with Ross. I thought Ross was her boyfriend; maybe Parker was just a friend. Not that it was any of my business.

I was in the shower when the bathroom door burst open.

"I got it!" Alisha cried.

"Got what?" I called back.

"A part in the stage production! Hurry up! Lisa and I are going out to celebrate, and you have to come with us!"

We ended up at the food court, each celebrating in our own way: me with a burger, Alisha with a chef salad, and Lisa with pizza. When you're working a summer job, celebrations are as inexpensive as you can make them.

"So what exactly will you do?" I asked.

"I'm not sure. They'll start teaching us the routines tomorrow. Basically, we come out on stage and sing and dance. You'll have to come watch a performance sometime."

"You must be really talented," Lisa said.

Alisha shook her head. "I don't think so. I think everyone else was just really bad. Some people just don't have a clue about how hard it is to perform."

"How long have you been dancing?" I asked.

"Since I was four."

"Wow! That's a long time."

"I really want to go to Hollywood someday. You have to commit early. So what job did you get?"

I stuck a French fry into ketchup, swirled it around. "I'm working in the gift shop."

"Oh, no," Lisa said. "Which gift shop?"

"Pick the worst one."

"Hansel and Gretel's?"

"Yep." I shook my head. "I got my costume today. How about you?"

"Carousel ride."

I was jealous. "That's my favorite."

"I figure after an hour of listening to that music, it won't be mine."

"Want to switch positions?"

She laughed. "No, Gretel."

Gosh, was that going to become my nickname? If so, I was already tired of it.

After dinner, we went back to our rooms. Jordan wasn't back yet. I watched a little TV, thanks to the fact that she'd brought one. Checked my e-mail. Read the joke about rednecks that Nick had forwarded to me. Sent a reply, "Ha-ha! Miss you." Then wrote a letter to Sarah about my day. Tried not to be disappointed that no one was online to flash me an IM.

I sat in my desk chair, looked out the window over the lake, and watched the way the moonlight sparkled over the water.

So tomorrow I'd pick up my costume and report to the Hansel and Gretel gift shop inside Storybook Land. It was a good thing I had a

boyfriend, because the only hotties I'd be seeing were overdressed tourists who were literally
hot and sweating. I might work with a Hansel,
but his costume would be as bad as mine, and
would definitely ruin any to-die-for factor
that might have been evident before said costume was put on. We'd be surrounded by
munchkins and their parents. No young cute
guy tourists would ever show their faces at
H & G's. Come to think of it, no girls my age
would show up, either.

I told myself that it didn't matter. I was
there to work, after all. But part of the appeal
of coming here was the opportunity to experience new things, meet new people. And just as
I was feeling really sorry for myself, I realized
that I'd met a lot of new people already. So I
was being silly.

The phone rang. Had to be for Jordan, but
since she wasn't here . . . let it ring.

But I was too weak. I picked up on the
third ring.

"Hello."

"Hey, Meg."

Parker. Gosh, I didn't like the way he

sounded. Like there were secrets shared between us.

"Megan," I corrected him.

"No, that voice doesn't go with a Megan."

The nerve of this guy. He didn't even know me and here he was . . . I couldn't deny that I was flattered.

"Jordan's not here."

"I know. She's on her way back."

"Then why did you call?"

"Your voice. It's been haunting me. What do you look like?"

"Listen, I have a boyfriend."

"Does he work at the park?"

"No."

"Where are you from?" he asked.

I stared harder out the window. Why was I answering this guy?

"Dallas."

"He's there. You're here. That has to be hard."

"Are you offering to fill in for him?"

He laughed, that deep rumble that shimmied through me. "If I were that obvious, I think you'd lose all respect for me."

"You've made the mistaken assumption that I had any respect for you to begin with."

He laughed again. Then he quieted suddenly, and all I could hear was the pounding of my heart.

"Dark hair," he said quietly.

"What?"

"You have dark hair."

"What does it matter?"

"Your voice sounds exotic."

"Well, I'm not. I'll tell Jordan you called."

"No, don't tell her. Like I said, I called to talk to you."

There was a strange shift in his voice that I couldn't quite identify.

"You don't want her to know you called me?"

"Let's just say that it would be better if she didn't know."

"I hear the key going into the lock."

"Then that's my cue to hang up. Sweet dreams."

And as quickly as a heartbeat he was gone.

I dropped the phone in the cradle just as Jordan walked into the room. My hands were shaking, and I didn't know why. I hadn't done anything wrong, but I felt like I was betraying my roommate and my boyfriend. How dumb was that?

"How was dinner?" I asked.

"Great. I love Parker so much. He's the best."

She loved Parker? I thought she loved Ross. Maybe she could love more than one guy at a time.

"He called." I couldn't stop myself from saying it. I didn't owe the guy anything and if she loved him but he was flirting with me . . . but then she had Ross . . .

"Parker?"

"Yeah."

"I wonder why he didn't call on my cell. I recharged it." She pulled her cell out of her pocket and for some reason I panicked.

"He just wanted to know if you got home safe. As soon as I heard your key in the door and told him you were here, he hung up."

She closed her phone. "Crazy guy. He worries about me so much. Overprotective. That's what he is. I'm going to take a shower and go to bed. Tomorrow is going to be a long day."

I was beginning to feel like it was going to be a long summer.

Only 54 Nick-less days to go, and counting. . . .

Chapter 6

"Remember: The customer is always right. No matter how old, how small, how grumpy."

Nancy (St. Augustine, FL) pressed the tips of her fingers against her cheeks, and twisted until her lips curled up. "And we always smile. It's hard to get upset with someone who's smiling at you."

Nancy managed H & G's. She had red hair, braided on either side of her head. Not even managers were exempt from the tortures of the theme park. And here in Storybook Land, we were all in costume. We actually had one Hansel in the store, and I decided it was way worse for a guy to be Hansel than for a girl to be Gretel. He had to be on someone's hate-this-guy list.

I cast a glance over at Patti. She rolled her

eyes. I so agreed with that assessment of our situation.

"Follow me and I'll show you how to work the register," Nancy said.

Pointing a scan gun didn't require a lot of skill. Neither did making change or bagging souvenirs. This was going to be an easy gig and no doubt boring as all get out. Patti and I spent the morning doing imaginary sales, then voiding them; practiced making change; and learned to run credit cards.

Around one o'clock, Nancy cut us loose. Patti and I changed out of our costumes, dropped them off, and started walking back to the dorm.

"Hey, since we only have a couple more days before things get crazy and we're working full shifts, you want to spend this afternoon with me on the rides?"

I grimaced. "I'm not really into thrill rides."

She stared at me. "You're kidding. Why are you working here, then?"

"Because I wanted to get away from home."

"But the whole point in being here is that you can ride the rides for free."

I shook my head. "I like the antique cars. And the carousel."

"Oh my God, I've heard of people like you."

"People like me?"

"Yeah, people who are irrationally afraid—"

"I'm not irrationally afraid. I just don't enjoy doing it."

"They have a guy, some famous psychiatrist who comes here every Wednesday and helps people get over their roller coaster phobias. You should sign up for a session."

"Why? I have no desire whatsoever to ride one, so why bother learning to do it?"

"Because you're afraid and you need to conquer your fear."

"I'm not afraid." Afraid was too tame a word for what I felt at the thought of even getting on a roller coaster. I'd ridden one once, with my dad. I'd buried my face against his arm and screamed during the entire ride. I was twelve. Hadn't been on one since.

I didn't like the heart-in-my-throat feeling, the sensation of plummeting. And I absolutely hated the cranking sound as the car went up the incline.

"Then go riding with me," Patti said.

We stepped out of the building into the sunshine.

"I can't. I really have a lot of stuff that I need to do."

"Like what?"

"I need to call my boyfriend before his shift starts tonight."

She narrowed her eyes. "Yeah, right. Well, I'm going to go ride Magnum Force. The guy who manages the controls there is totally hot."

I smiled. "So it's not that you're a roller coaster fanatic. It's that you're hoping to hook up with someone."

"You know it. Later, girlfriend!"

I watched her walk away. I guess it did seem a little insane for someone who didn't like thrill rides to work at a place known for them.

I was going to head to the dorm, but then changed my mind. I would do a ride after all.

I went to the carousel. I don't know what it is about carousels. I love the old-time feel of them. The mirrors, the gold, the glitter. The music. And I always ride on a horse that goes up and down. Of course, I was probably the oldest one on the carousel that afternoon, but what the heck. I could live dangerously every now and then.

I actually stayed in the park until it closed, which for two more days would be seven in the evening. When I got back to the room, Jordan was dressed to kill in low-rider jeans, spike-heeled boots, and a clinging spaghetti-strap tank top that revealed her belly button ring. Her hair was spiked out in all directions.

"Hot date?" I asked.

She slapped her forehead. "I am such a dunce. I forgot to tell you. Parker is having a party tonight. Wanna come?"

"No, thanks."

"Why not?"

I thought about the phone call last night. The fact that he spent time with her, she loved him, then he called me . . .

"I'm exhausted. I spent the afternoon on the rides."

"Oh!" She squealed. "Did you ride Magnum Force?"

I don't know what possessed me not to confess that my rides had been the three different carousels, the taxis, and the teacups. "You bet."

"Isn't it awesome?"

"Totally."

"Did you ride in the first car?"

"No." Don't know why I chose at that moment not to lie.

"Oh, you have got to ride in the front. It is a totally different experience. No one to block your view as you're hurtling along the rails."

"I've got all summer. No sense in doing everything at once."

"That's true. Sure you don't want to come with me tonight?"

"I'm sure."

"His roomie is twenty-one. There will be booze."

"I'm not twenty-one."

"So? He doesn't card, you know."

"I have to be at costume at eight in the morning."

"So?"

"Thanks so much, Jordan, but I just can't."

"All right. Don't wait up."

She slung her purse over her shoulder and was gone.

I sat on my bed. Another exciting night.

It actually turned out not to be too bad. Zoe, our floor monitor, knocked on my door about eight.

"You the only one left on the floor?" she asked.

"I guess so. I haven't seen my suitemates, and my roomie went to a party."

"Brilliant! Come on down and join me, then. I just called for a pizza, and they delivered a large instead of a small."

Her room was awesome. Painted pink instead of white like ours. She had posters of England on the walls: Stonehenge, a guard standing outside Buckingham Palace.

"How did you end up here?" I asked, just before I bit into the mushroom pizza.

"Came on holiday with my parents a couple of years ago. Loved it! So I came back the next summer. Worked the rides. The summer after that I worked tickets. This year I'm bossing people around."

"You mean on the floor."

"No, luvie. I oversee some of the ride crews. I'm the hall monitor, so they don't take anything out of my paycheck for staying in the dorm. And I might as well be, I'm here anyway. So how are you liking your position?"

"You mean as Gretel?"

"Oh, God." She looked like she might hurl her pizza. "You're a Gretel?"

I nodded.

"So sorry, Megan."

I smiled. "It's not that bad."

"It's bloody awful is what it is. Little ones crying 'cuz they can't have a toy. It's my least favorite place."

"Thanks a lot. At least it's air-conditioned."

"It is that."

She'd left her door open, so as girls returned for the night, they stopped by. She had lots of warnings for everyone—don't look for a summer love, keep cool with the guys, don't end the summer with a broken heart.

By the time I left her room, I didn't know if I was glad or not that I'd come here for the summer.

The phone woke me. Not the soft ring of my cell, but the clanging of the dorm phone. I groaned, buried my head under the pillow, then decided that since it was after one it could be Jordan calling with an emergency.

Groggily, I scrambled for the phone. "Hello?"

"Hey, Roomie!"

She sounded totally wasted.

"Jordan?"

"Listen, I missed curfew so I'm going to sleep in Parker's bed tonight."

More information than I needed to know.

"Whatever."

"I just didn't want you worrying."

But I was worried a little. I mean what if he'd deliberately gotten her drunk to take advantage of her?

"Jordan, be careful, okay?"

"Always." She giggled. "I'll see . . . oh, wait. Parker wants to talk to you."

"Why me? Jordan, no—"

"Hey."

Okay, I *so* did not like the way that his voice sent pleasant chills through me, and I was a little angry that he had flirted with me last night. Angry for Jordan, not about me. I had a boyfriend, and I wasn't interested in Parker, but he needed to treat my roomie better.

"Did you get her drunk?" I asked pointedly.

"No, she did that all on her own. She said she invited you to come to the party. So why didn't you come?"

His voice was lazy, sultry, and quiet. I could hear people and music in the background. Why hadn't I wanted to go to a party? Why had I chosen to spend the night eating pizza in the dorm? Because just this guy's voice had me thinking things that I shouldn't be thinking. I thought about his stupid voice more than I thought about Nick.

"I'm not into the party scene." What a lie. As a rule, I loved parties, but how could I have fun at a party when my boyfriend was hundreds of miles away? It seemed like cheating or something.

"It's not a wild party—"

"Jordan sounded pretty wild."

"Jordan is always wild. She's all about having fun."

"So I gathered."

"What about you, Megan? You like to have fun?"

"Well, duh? Yeah!"

"So why didn't you come to the party?"

"I already answered that."

"Except that you lied."

I stuck out my tongue, even though no one could see.

"Look, I need to go," I said.

"Why do I get the impression you don't like me?"

"I don't know you well enough not to like you," I said. "But shouldn't you be spending time with the people who are there?"

"Yeah, probably. The next time I have a party, you should come, okay?"

"I'll think about it."

"But you won't come, will you?"

"Probably not."

"Why?"

Because his voice intrigued me and that was oh so dangerous.

"Because I have a boyfriend."

"So? We could be just friends."

"Yeah, right. That's why you keep calling to talk to me. Because you want to be *friends*. How do you think Jordan would feel about that?"

He released a low groan. "Yeah, that could get awkward."

"That's what I thought. 'Night, Parker."

I hung up before he could say anything else. I was rooming with the good-time gal.

It took me a long time to go back to sleep. And when I did, I dreamed about Nick. Only whenever he talked, he sounded like Parker.

Only 53 Nick-less days to go, and counting. . . .

Chapter 7

"Okay, so tomorrow is the big day, right?" Patti asked after we'd changed out of our costumes and were heading out of the building.

"That's what they say."

We stepped out into the bright sunshine.

"You sure wouldn't know it by our boring day. I hope we have more customers tomorrow."

All during our shift at H & G's, we'd stood within the circle of the counter with four cash registers, only one being used. She'd rung people up, I'd bagged the items. Totally boring.

"You should watch what you wish for," I told her.

"I'm wishing for something to make the time go faster. Don't suppose you've overcome your roller coaster phobia."

"It's not a phobia."

"So today you'll ride with me?"

"No, today I'm going to sit out by the pool, enjoy the sunshine."

"All right, then, I'll see you tomorrow."

She walked off, and I headed toward the entrance. It was actually starting to get a little more crowded along the midway. It was Friday and people were coming in early for the weekend. The park would actually stay open until ten o'clock tonight, midnight tomorrow. Tomorrow I would start working the late shift, so I could sleep in, which was great because I am not a morning person.

I edged around a little kid who was running to get somewhere, his mother chasing after him, and knocked up against a guy.

"Oh, sorry," I said, embarrassed but continuing on.

Someone grabbed my arm and spun me around. I found myself staring into gorgeous green eyes, sparkling eyes, amused eyes.

"Megan?"

I swallowed hard, almost shook my head

no, mostly because I couldn't believe who I might be staring at. "Parker?"

He slowly grinned. "Yeah. I recognized your voice."

"I recognized yours, too."

He had black hair, cut pretty short. I imagined that working on the roller coasters, he'd want to be as cool as possible. He was wearing jeans, a black T-shirt, and a yellow Livestrong bracelet.

"I got your hair wrong," he said.

I found myself self-consciously touching it. After I'd changed out of my costume, I'd unraveled my braids, brushed my hair, pulled it back, and used a clip to hold it in place off my shoulders. No way was I going to walk around off-duty looking like Gretel.

"I pegged you for a brunette," he continued. "But it's a golden brown. It suits you. The eyes, though, brown and mysterious, I got those right. So are you done with your shift?"

I nodded. "Yeah, heading back to the dorm."

"Me, too." He shook his head, his grin growing. "Finished with my shift, not heading to the dorm. Want to go get some Dippin' Dots?"

"Look—"

"I know you've got a boyfriend, but I don't know that many people around here—"

"Hey, Parker!" a guy called out as he strode by.

"Hey, Matt!" Parker cleared his throat. "Okay, I know a few people, but I believe people are experiences that we need to experience. So come on, what's ten minutes of your time?"

What was ten minutes of my time when I thought my roommate had slept with him, and he seemed to be flirting with me?

Decisions . . . decisions.

Say no and remain mysterious, have him keep calling and trying to get to know me better.

Say yes and be as dull as possible so he leaves me alone.

"Sure, why not?" I said.

I didn't think it was possible, but his smile grew even broader. "Great! Come on, it's this way."

I wrinkled my brow. "Are you sure, because I thought it was that way," I said, pointing in the opposite direction.

"This is my third year here. Believe me, I know where the Dippin' Dots cart is. I'm addicted to them."

I considered arguing, but the park was huge. He must know where the cart was and I was just confused.

"Okay, lead the way."

"So, what job did you get?" he asked, glancing over at me.

"What would be the worst job imaginable?"

"Hansel and Gretel gift shop."

I arched my brow.

He looked like he was in pain. "Oh, man! Bummer. So what, you have experience working a cash register?"

I hadn't even considered that. I had put on my application that I'd worked in a clothing store my junior year. So yeah, maybe it was my experience working in a store or maybe it was as Patti and I surmised. . . .

"I was thinking it was my hair."

"I can't tell with it clipped back. How long is it?"

"Past my shoulders." I glanced over at him

impatiently. "Shouldn't we have reached Dippin' Dots by now?"

He shook his head. "Nah, it's just up here."

Only I didn't see it, and I was beginning to suspect that we were taking the long route and that I'd been right to begin with.

"Hey, Parker," another guy said in passing.

"John."

"You sure know a lot of people," I said.

"They're just my crew."

"Your crew?"

"Yeah, I oversee Magnum Force."

I remembered Jordan mentioning that he had to ride the roller coaster every morning.

"You been on it?" he asked.

"Nope."

"Want to ride it after we have our Dippin' Dots? I have a cut-to-the-front-of-the-line pass."

"No, thanks."

"Why not? It's a tight ride."

"I'm just not into roller coasters."

"What's not to be into? The thrill of the speed, the plummets, the loops—"

"It just doesn't appeal to me, okay?"

"Are you afraid?"

"I'm not afraid."

"There's a guy—"

"Who comes on Wednesday. I know. My friend Patti told me. But it's not a phobia. It's just something I have no interest in."

"How can you not be interested?"

Why couldn't people just accept my decision and let it go?

"Do you ride the carousel?" I asked.

"Not since I was about eight."

"Okay, that's your choice. My choice is to ride the carousel, not the roller coaster."

"It's not the same. If you asked, I'd ride the carousel. As a matter of fact, after we eat our ice cream, we'll ride the carousel."

I stopped walking, put my hands on my hips, and glared at him. "I agreed to the Dippin' Dots, but not a ride. And speaking of the Dippin' Dots, I don't think you know where the cart is."

"I know where it is. We're about halfway there."

I stared at him, unable to believe it. "If we'd gone the other direction, we'd already be there, wouldn't we?"

"Yeah, but then we wouldn't have had as

much time to talk."

I scoffed. "I can't believe you did that."

"Why? Your voice fascinates me. It's so smoky sounding."

"It sounds like I'm a smoker."

"No, it doesn't. My Uncle Joe is a smoker, hacking cough and everything. You don't sound like him. You sound like"—he shrugged—"I just like the way it sounds, wanted to learn if there are other things about you that I might like."

I laughed lightly. "But it doesn't matter. I have a boyfriend."

Holding out his arms, he looked around. "Where? I don't see him."

"You're too much, you know that?" Turning, I started to walk away. He grabbed my arm again. I jerked free. "Look—"

"Okay, I'm sorry. I know a shortcut."

"Right. I thought *this* was supposed to be a shortcut."

"It was a shortcut to my getting to know you."

At least he was honest.

"So sue me," he added, not looking at all

sheepish, but somehow managing to defuse my anger. "Come on, I'm paying for the Dippin' Dots. You can't beat that."

"The ice cream, that's all," I said.

"Scout's honor."

I narrowed my eyes at him. "And you know a real shortcut."

"Yep, follow me."

I fell into step beside him. I couldn't help but be a little flattered that he'd gone to so much trouble. Or that he liked my voice. And he did know a shortcut. We slipped into a gate marked EMPLOYEES ONLY, walked along what looked like an alley between some of the rides, and when we came out on the other side, there was the cart we'd been looking for.

I ordered strawberry, he ordered chocolate. I didn't argue when he paid. I figured he owed me.

He pointed with the hand holding the cup of Dippin' Dots, the other holding a spoon, toward a bench. "Wanna sit?"

"Sure."

I sat on the bench, and he sat beside me.

A couple of people called out to him as they walked by.

"You know a lot of people," I said.

"I'm a likable guy."

"So, Jordan said you live in a house on the lake."

"Yep, a buddy and I are house-sitting over the summer. A guy we met last year needed someone to look after his place this summer, so he made us a great deal. Couldn't afford a house on the lake otherwise."

"That's a lot of responsibility."

"I live for responsibility."

He leaned forward, planting his elbows on his thighs, dipping into his cup of tiny frozen ice cream balls. I thought about asking him exactly what his relationship was with Jordan. I mean, it seemed odd to me that she'd slept with him, but here he was spending time with me. I certainly didn't want to be the reason that they broke up. That would make for a very awkward roommate situation. Worse even than being around Mom and Sarah while they fought about the wedding.

"You like watching movies?" he asked.

"Who doesn't?"

"Some people don't. What's your favorite?"

I smiled. "Are you playing twenty questions?"

"Just trying to get to know you a little better. So what's your favorite movie?"

Seemed like a harmless question. "*Titanic*."

He cringed.

"What's wrong with *Titanic*?"

"Don't get me wrong. Loved the special effects, but it was just a little too mushy."

"Well, I loved it. Your favorite is probably *Night of the Living Dead*."

"*Blade Runner*."

I shook my head. "I thought that one was strange."

"It's kind of a tech-noir movie, and I appreciate film noir more after I sat through a class on the subject."

I shook my head again, feeling a little dense. "I have no clue what film noir is."

He grinned. "It's a style of black-and-white movies that became popular after World War II. Detective movies where the filming style seemed really dark. That semester we watched all the old classics during class."

"A class where you watch movies. Sounds tough."

"Yeah, it's a rough life. I'm majoring in film. The danger there is that you stop watching movies for the enjoyment factor, but for the critique factor. What worked, what didn't? But I discovered that if I go to a movie with a girl, I'm less likely to go into critique mode."

I was shaking my head and grinning.

"What?" he asked.

"I see where this is leading."

"Maybe we could catch a movie sometime."

"I don't think so."

"Why not?"

"Boyfriend factor."

"It wouldn't have to be a date."

"Jordan factor?"

"As much as I love Jordan she is so not a factor."

What a jerk! But for some reason I didn't say it to his face. Maybe because I was disappointed that someone as good looking as he was, someone who seemed so nice, could turn out to be a total creep.

"Sorry. But I'm not interested. At all." I tapped the bottom of my empty cup. "Gotta go."

I stood up and tossed my cup in the trash.

"Thanks," he said.

I looked over at him. He was still sitting there, elbows on his knees, his ice cream melting. He didn't look like a guy who was trying to cheat on his girlfriend. I guess it was true what they said: Looks can be deceiving.

Of course, Jordan had Parker and Ross. Plus some guy named Cole who claimed to love her. Maybe they were just all into love without commitment. I wasn't.

"For what?" I asked.

"For hanging out with me."

"We weren't really hanging out."

"Whatever. Think about coming to my place the next time we have a party."

"Do you have a lot of parties?"

"Oh, yeah, and every Wednesday night we have a hump party . . . and it's not what you think. It's to help us get through the middle-of-the-week hump."

"I'll think about it."

"Great."

I didn't know why I felt bad walking away. I didn't know if it was guilt because he was involved with Jordan and I was involved with Nick. Or if it was just leaving him there, with a lie. Because I wasn't going to think about it.

If I felt this guilty just talking to him, getting ice cream with him, how much worse would I feel if partied with him?

Only 50 Nick-less days to go, and counting. . . .

Chapter 8

"I'm sure that my son did not eat a little gingerbread man," the woman standing in front of my cash register said.

The fact that the five-year-old monster still had crumbs at the corner of his mouth seemed to say otherwise to me, but the customer is always right, so smiling brightly, I removed the cookie from her total.

"That'll be $12.56," I said.

She began laying coins on the counter. I wanted to scream. There was a long line behind her with harried parents and tired kids, and she'd dipped into her piggy bank. I wanted to tell her to forget it, but I started helping her count.

She slapped at my hand. "Don't touch my money."

"Yes, ma'am."

An eternity later, I was finally saying, "Next!"

"When's your break?"

How could I have not noticed Parker standing in line? And how long had he been standing there?

"Not soon enough," I said.

He stepped aside without me having to prod him to get out of the way, and I took care of the next customer. At least this one was using a credit card.

It had been nonstop customers from the moment I came into H & G. Although we were open until midnight, people with kids were getting ready to leave the park, and each and every one of them needed souvenirs. It was a constant stream of customers.

I felt a tap on my shoulder and glanced back. It was Nancy. "Time for your break."

I wanted to hug her. "Great! Thank you."

I slipped through the narrow opening in between the two sections of the counter and started for the door. I barely noticed when Parker fell into step beside me.

"I have to sit down," I said, as soon as we were outside.

"Over here."

I didn't protest when he took my arm and led me to a small table, a pint-sized table — because we were, after all, in Storybook Land — and my knees touched the tabletop when I sat in the small chair. I put my elbows on the table and dropped my head into my hands. I just wanted to go to sleep and it was only seven o'clock.

"Here."

I looked up. Parker had set a cup of lemonade and a huge salty pretzel in front of me.

"Thanks." I tore off a piece of the pretzel, popped it into my mouth, and chewed. It was heavenly. "I didn't even realize I was hungry."

"You usually don't. At least not at first."

"This is insane."

"It'll get worse before the summer is over."

I sipped the lemonade. "I don't see how it can."

"Trust me, it will."

I took another bite of pretzel. "What are you doing here, anyway?"

Shrugging, he tore off some pretzel and ate it. He was in his uniform: khaki cargo shorts, red polo shirt, name tag. Parker (Los Angeles, CA).

So he probably wasn't Jordan's summer boyfriend. They probably knew each other from school or the neighborhood or something. I remembered that first day, how excited she'd been that he'd called. Maybe she'd come here to be with him. But then what was Ross to her?

They obviously had a connection.

"What are you thinking?" he asked.

Now it was my turn to shrug, shake my head, and lie. "That I never knew eight hours could seem so long."

He grinned, reached for the lemonade, and took a sip. The park didn't use straws because too many ended up on the ground and the maintenance crew had to sweep them up. Still it seemed intimate that we were sharing a drink, even if he wasn't using the side of the cup that I'd used.

"So how is it at Magnum Force?" I asked.

"Unbelievable. When I left, the wait in line was an hour and a half."

"I can think of better things to do with my time than wait in line."

"Me, too. Listen, some of us are getting together at my place after the park closes, just to unwind. Thought you might want to join us."

"You know, I really think I'm going to be too tired."

He studied me a couple of seconds, then said, "Okay." He did a *rat-a-tat-tat* on the table with his palms. "I need to get back to work."

He stood and stepped back.

"Thanks again for the rescue," I said.

"Sure thing."

"Maybe after I've adjusted to the schedule . . ."

He nodded and smiled. "Let me know if you think of anything that I can do to help you adjust."

Before I could respond, he'd spun on his heel and was walking away.

What in the world made me say that, made me offer him any kind of hope at all?

In the end, I was actually grateful that I had said no to the party. I was completely wiped out.

Or so I thought. But it was just my body that was exhausted. My mind was traveling about as fast as Magnum Force. I couldn't get it to slow down.

I lay in bed, staring in the darkness, the sound of the cash register still ringing in my ears.

No, wait, it wasn't the cash register. It was the phone. I reached over and grabbed it. "Hello?"

"Hey."

Parker. Why was I not surprised?

"Listen, Jordan crashed in my bed, so she's staying here tonight. I didn't want you to worry about her."

"I'm not her keeper. And listen, Parker, stop bothering me, okay?"

I hung up before he could answer. I knew it was totally irrational on my part to be upset, but could the guy be any more of a player?

I reached for my cell phone and punched a number. Nick picked up on the second ring.

"Megan? What's wrong?"

"Did I wake you?"

"No."

He was lying. I could tell by his voice. It had that just-woke-up rasp to it, but I loved him for trying not to make me feel guilty.

"I know it's late, but I needed to hear your voice," I said.

"I'm glad you called. I needed to hear your voice, too. How is it there?"

"Busy." I'd called him two nights ago and told him about the position I'd been given. "Lots of little kids wanting souvenirs, crying because they're tired. Typical stuff. My feet hurt."

"Mine, too."

"How are things there?"

"Frustrating. We got this new waitress— Tess. I'm supposed to train her, and she thinks she already knows it all, so when I try to tell her something, she won't listen."

"Then leave her to it. Let her make a fool of herself."

"But it'll fall on me and I'll get chewed out. I wish you were here. I really need a distraction."

I wasn't certain that I liked being called a distraction.

"A distraction?"

"You know. Something to take my mind off work. I miss you, Megan. I miss kissing you, talking to you, holding you."

"I miss you, too, Nick. We can still talk, even if we can't kiss or hold."

"I know, but it's not the same when I can't look at you."

I tried really hard not to think about the phone calls that Parker had made before he even knew what I looked like. He'd been content to just hear my voice, to talk with me. So unfair. Parker was a player. The calls hadn't meant anything, other than the fact that at that precise moment when he was talking, he wasn't giving attention to Jordan.

"So?" Nick said.

I shook my head. "I'm sorry. I must have dozed off."

"What? Am I boring or something?"

"No, Nick, I'm just tired. What did you say?"

"I said that I'm counting the days until you come home."

"Really?"

"Yeah. Forty-nine to go. I'm saving up my kisses."

I laughed lightly. "You'd better be."

"I was thinking that when the summer is over we could do something special."

"Like what?"

"Like go somewhere for the weekend, just the two of us. You know?"

Yeah, I did know, sorta. "Like my mom's going to go for that."

"She let you go up there for the whole summer."

"Yeah, but there are people here watching over me, so she doesn't think I could get into any trouble."

"How close do they watch?"

"Not very."

"So . . . if I came up for a visit . . ."

"I'd see a lot of you, Nick, when I wasn't working."

He sighed. "But I don't have any vacation days. Since I'm part-time."

"It's a nice thought, though, isn't it? That we could be together up here without any parents around?"

"Yeah. Who knows? Maybe I'll go AWOL."

"If you're going to do that and risk your job, then you could have come up here with me for the summer."

"I didn't know I'd miss you this badly, Megan. I mean, I knew I'd miss you, but I'm miserable without you."

It seemed kinda mean to feel good that he was miserable. Shouldn't I feel just as miserable? Only I didn't, but it was just because I was so busy. I was working full-time. Nick had more time on his hands.

We talked for another half an hour, and when we said good-bye, he was making kissing noises, which made me laugh and made me miss him. Made me miserable.

Only 49 Nick-less days to go, and counting. . . .

Chapter 9

Monday was my day off, and I was so incredibly ready for it. Strangely, I woke up to find my roommate sleeping in her bed. She must have come in after I'd already been asleep. I wondered why she didn't just move in with Parker. She'd stayed over twice now, and had gone to his place for dinner again last night, so they were obviously serious.

I tried to be quiet getting out of bed, but she rolled over and looked at me. Smiled. "Hey!"

I'd never known anyone who actually woke up happy.

"Hi," I muttered. First thing in the morning wasn't when I was at my best.

"I am totally bummed," she said. "It's my

day off and Ross has to work. I can't believe that his day off is tomorrow and he couldn't find anyone to swap with him—"

She was back to Ross now? Was that why she'd slept in her own bed?

"And it's so unfair. The whole point of us coming here was so we could be together."

"What about Parker?" I asked.

"What about him?"

"You slept over—"

"Yeah, so? What has that got to do with anything?"

I shrugged. "Apparently nothing."

We obviously had a different view on commitment. I mean, I didn't even want to hang around with the guy, even nonseriously, because I had a boyfriend far, far away.

Suddenly, she sat up. "So you want to go to the mall with me? They had some of the cutest little shops, and I've been dying to get back there, but it's no fun shopping alone, you know? So how 'bout it, roomie? You and me, shopping 'til we drop?"

The other option was to spend the day alone lying on the sand or by the pool. Decisions,

decisions . . . what the heck? I was ready to get away.

"Sure, I'd love to go the mall." Not that I had any money to spend, but maybe I'd find something that would make a unique wedding present for Sarah, and I wanted to send something to Nick so he'd know I was thinking about him.

"Awesome!" Jordan said. "We'll have oodles of fun!"

The mall was like a thousand other malls in a thousand other cities, and the fact that it was so familiar made me feel less homesick. Though until that moment, I hadn't even realized that I *was* homesick.

Not that I had a lot of time to focus on home, not while shopping with Jordan. She was incredible. I'd never known anyone with so much energy or such shopping skills. She seemed able to take in an entire display with a single glance.

"Oh, look at this, isn't this cute?" she asked, pointing to a pink halter with "YES, IT'S ALL ABOUT ME" glittering on it. "I've got to have this." She peered over at me. "Parker is always telling me that not everything is about me. And that is just so wrong."

So she was planning to still see Parker. Otherwise, why buy it?

"We should find one for you," she said. "What sentiment fits you? Princess? Nah. Spoiled? I don't think so. Too Hot to Handle? Yeah, that would do it."

She turned to me, holding out the red top that she'd decided suited me.

I laughed. "I'm not too hot to handle."

"It's the closest thing I can find." She shook it at me. "Come on. It's just for fun. You can wear it to Parker's hump party."

"I'm not even sure I'm going."

"Why not? I know he won't mind. He told me to invite my roomie and my suitemates."

So he hadn't told her that he'd issued me a personal invitation? Wasn't that interesting? Like he really didn't want her knowing that he knew me.

Of course he didn't want her to know. He'd already hinted a couple of times not to mention when he'd called or when he'd shown up at

H & G's. Although he hadn't come by yesterday, and the awful thing was, I'd kept looking for him. But he'd obviously taken the hint when I'd told him that I didn't want him bothering me anymore. So now he was going to let Jordan do the bothering.

"I think I'm working Wednesday," I said.

"Well, if you're not, you can come. And even if you are, the park closes at ten during the week. Plenty of time to party. Oh, look at these shorts. I've got to have them."

By the time we were finished, we'd eaten lunch at the food court, Jordan had bought something in nearly every store—she'd spent way more than we'd make in earnings that week—and I'd bought the Too Hot to Handle shirt only because she was going to buy it for me if I didn't, and I didn't want her spending her money on me. I had a feeling that Jordan saw money the same way that she saw guys— disposable.

Not that it was any of my business.

I didn't find anything special for Sarah or Nick.

"So how is it working at H & G?" Jordan

asked as we were walking to her car.

"Not too bad."

"You hear from your boyfriend much?"

"We talk at least once a day, usually before I go to bed. And he's always forwarding me all these jokes through e-mail. Each e-mail's subject heading is like a hostage watch or something: day 3 without Megan, day 5 without Megan."

"That's sweet!"

"It's so negative, though, like looking at a glass of milk and saying it's half empty. My subject headings are forty-seven days 'til I'm with Nick, forty-five days 'til I'm with Nick."

"The anticipation, the countdown. I'm so with you. Positive vibes to get you through the separation. It's a shame he's not here. Even seeing him a little bit would be better than not seeing him at all."

She popped the trunk and dropped her packages inside. I put my single sack in there as well. Then we got in the car. She put the key in the ignition, turned it . . . nothing.

She looked over at me like I'd done something to the car. "It won't start."

"Maybe you didn't turn it far enough."

She tried again. Nada. Zilch.

"Great! Just great!" She searched around in her mammoth-sized purse and pulled out her cell phone, punched a button, waited . . .

"Hey! I've got a problem."

I tried not to listen as she explained what was happening. It seemed kinda nosey. When she ended the call, she said, "Parker will be here as soon as he can."

Parker. Great. This could get awkward.

"Let's wait outside where it's a little cooler," she said.

We sat on the hood of her car, my stomach knotting more tightly as the minutes went by. I knew it was ridiculous to worry about what might happen when Parker finally arrived. Would he acknowledge me? Had he told Jordan that he'd called me a couple of times, that we'd shared ice cream, that he'd taken his break with me?

Did any of it mean anything? It couldn't. They'd slept together afterward. He was just being . . . friendly to her roommate.

A black Mustang pulled up beside us, and Jordan slid off the hood. I didn't think it was possible, but my stomach knotted up even more tightly when Parker got out of the car.

They greeted each other, then he looked at me, and even though he was wearing sunglasses, I had the impression that it was an extremely penetrating look and my discomfort with the situation intensified.

"This is my roomie, Megan," Jordan said.

"Yeah, we've met," Parker said.

"When?" Jordan asked.

"Long story. What's wrong with your car?" he asked impatiently.

"It's broken."

He scowled. She shrugged and held up her key. "It won't start, doesn't make any noise."

"Great. Probably the battery."

"Probably. Why don't you let me take your car while you figure it out? Megan and I have things we need to do."

"Like what?"

"None of your business. But let's do a vehicle swap, and we'll fix you dinner tonight."

"Who's we?" he asked, but he was looking at me, probably because I was slowly sliding off the hood, wondering what Jordan was about to get me into.

"Me and Megan." She glanced over at me. "You don't mind, do you?"

How could I say no without seeming ungrateful?

"Sure." If I'd used a longer word, my response would have been a stammer.

"So see?" Jordan said to Parker. "You get a free meal out of the deal."

"I'm not sure that makes it worth it."

"Sure it does," she said. "Pop the trunk so we can get our bags out."

Hardly knowing what else to say or do, I walked around to the back of the car to get my bag. Parker opened the trunk.

"Good Lord!" he said when he saw all the bags inside.

He reached in at the same time that I reached in and we bumped heads.

"Sorry," we said at the same time, each of us rubbing our respective heads.

"I just have the one little bag," I said, pointing and reaching, but he was reaching too and somehow with us both grabbing it, the shirt fell out.

"Sorry," he said again, quicker at grabbing it than I was.

It unfolded as he was lifting it out. Then he was staring at it, a grin forming over his face, before looking at me.

I snatched it from his fingers. "It was Jordan's idea."

His grin grew. "But you're going to be the one wearing it. Are you too hot to handle?"

"You'll never know."

His grin faded and I bit my lower lip. Why had I said that? Why was I so touchy whenever he was around?

Because he belonged to Jordan, but didn't act like it, and I belonged to Nick, but had a hard time remembering that whenever this guy was around.

"Sorry," I mumbled again, but I don't know if he heard me. He was too busy gathering up all of Jordan's bags and carrying them to his car.

And now I was going to have to spend the evening fixing this guy supper?

Could life get any more complicated?

Chapter 10

*I*t could.

Or if not more complicated, it was definitely beginning to feel out of control.

The reason Jordan had so desperately wanted to swap cars with Parker was because she had an appointment to get a manicure and pedicure, and since we were running late, she didn't have time to drop me off at the dorm. So by default, since they had an opening, I got a manicure and pedicure as well.

The place where we went was called the Salons of Indulgence. It was actually a lot of little rooms in this main building, and different things happened in different rooms. And of course, Jordan had appointments lined up in several of the rooms.

"You don't have to get an eyebrow waxing," she said after we were finished at the nail salon. Then she leaned toward me. "But what can it hurt? Just a little more shaping than you have now."

I stood by the doorway and watched as she laid back in the recliner and the woman waxed her brows. I'd never actually had a waxing done. But it looked relatively painless.

When Jordan was finished, I decided what the heck. Plucking my eyebrows was a tedious chore anyway, so I took a turn.

Ow! I was wrong. It *did* hurt! And the reason it hurt was because she'd removed a good portion of my eyebrows.

I stared in the mirror when she was finished.

"You have a natural arch," she said with an accent from some Scandanavian country. "You weren't taking advantage of it. See how much bigger your eyes look now? The men will be dazzled."

"I don't need to dazzle men," I grumbled. "I have a boyfriend."

"Then he will be charmed."

"She's right," Jordan said. "Your eyes really do stand out now."

"My brows are still tingling."

"That'll stop soon, and if it doesn't, you can put some ice on them when we get back to the dorm. But honestly, next week, it'll hurt even less."

"Next week?"

"Sure," she said. "Monday maintenance is a weekly ritual for me. Since we're both off, you're more than welcome to come along, only next time we'll make appointments for you."

Monday maintenance? Geez.

"Once a month I do hair, facial, and massage," she added.

I shook my head. "Jordan, I can't afford to do this weekly. A haircut and an occasional manicure are really about all my budget can handle."

"Daddy gave me a credit card to use on anything I wanted. I can use it to pay for your stuff, too."

Was she crazy?

"Thanks, Jordan, but I'm not going to have your dad pay for my stuff."

"Why not?"

I couldn't believe she was asking.

"Because I believe in paying my own way."

"He won't mind, Megan. Money is so not an object with him."

"Well, it's an object with me. I'll join you when I can, but not every week."

"Okay," she said, a little sadness in her voice, "but if you change your mind . . . he said I was supposed to use the card to have fun, and spending time with you is fun."

"If your dad is paying for so much, why are you even working this summer?" I asked, hoping that I didn't sound rude.

"The experience. I don't want to be too spoiled. Besides, it's nice to have money of my own, you know?"

Yeah, I knew, but hanging around with Jordan, I wasn't going to hold on to it for long.

I'd barely dropped my stuff on my bed when Jordan announced that we didn't have much time to get ready.

"We need to go grocery shopping for tonight's dinner," she said before disappearing into the bathroom.

I heard the shower. What a tornado of activity!

But she was also a lot of fun, in a frenzied kind of way.

I thought about changing into the shirt I'd bought today, but decided it conveyed a message that I definitely didn't want Parker taking the wrong way. Especially since he'd already seen it.

I tried to think of an excuse to get out of helping with the dinner, without looking weird, but there was no way around it. Any excuse was a definite show of weirdness.

So after Jordan got out of the shower, I had my turn. Put on a light application of makeup, stared at myself in the mirror. Did a change to the shape of my eyebrows really make that much difference in the way that I looked?

I looked, gosh, I didn't know. Prettier?

Maybe it was the dark green of my tank top. Couldn't be the white of my shorts. But something sure made me look different. I decided to leave my hair loose, hanging around my face. Maybe it would detract from the radical change in my eyebrows. Did guys even really notice eyebrows?

On the way to Parker's, we stopped at this little grocery store. Jordan knew everything about Parker. That he only ate dark meat chicken, never white, which was important because we were going to make chicken and rice. He ate wheat rolls, again, never white. Kernel corn, never creamed. Unsweetened tea, never sweetened. Plain brownies, never double chocolate or iced or chunky chocolate.

"If it weren't for his love of roller coasters," she said, "the guy would be totally dull."

I almost told her I didn't think he was dull at all. But if she thought he was, why did she hang out with him? But I kept my opinion and curiosity to myself.

After we finished shopping, we drove over to his place. It was only about fifteen minutes from the dorm, but the setting was totally awesome. The house, like a few others that I could see, was set back along the lake, massive trees in front. It was a log cabin with a wide porch that wrapped around the front and sides. Each side had a couple of wicker rockers.

It was an incredibly peaceful place. No wonder Jordan spent so much time here. It was far away from the madness of the theme park. I couldn't hear the roller coasters or the screaming riders or the crying kids. As I stepped out of the car, I couldn't hear anything except the water lapping at the shore and the breeze rustling through the trees.

"Come on," Jordan said.

"What about the groceries?" I asked.

"The guys'll get them."

I followed her toward the house. A tall, blond guy in a dark T-shirt stepped onto the porch.

Jordan hopped up on the porch and hugged him. "This is Cole."

Cole, who had called the first night and declared his love for Jordan, lived with Parker, whom she slept with?

"You must be the roommate," he said to me.

"Oh, I'm sorry," Jordan said. "Yep, she's my roomie. Don't you love what she's done with herself today?"

"Jordan—" I began.

"And what is that?" a deep voice asked.

I turned toward Parker. He'd come up to the side of the porch. He was wearing a black T-shirt and jeans, his hands dirty with grease. How could anyone that dirty look that sexy?

"If you can't tell, I'm not going to tell you," Jordan said. "Did you get my car fixed?"

"Yeah. I had to replace the battery. But when was the last time you changed your oil?"

My roommate shrugged, looking a little guilty when she did it.

"Geez, Jordan, it's no wonder you have so much car trouble."

"But at least I have you to fix it. Will you guys get the groceries out of the car?"

She grabbed my arm. "Come on. I'll show you around while they do that."

The house was even better inside. Lots of leather furniture and brightly colored cushions and large windows in every room so we could look out onto the lake.

By the time we got to the kitchen, the groceries had been delivered. It was an open, cheery room.

Jordan walked to the oven and turned it on. "Let's get started."

It was really a pretty easy recipe. Chicken in a casserole dish, rice over the chicken, soup over the rice. Into the oven it all went, which left us with a couple of cans of corn to heat up and some rolls to bake. She worked on those while I hand-stirred the brownie mix.

I walked to the window and gazed out on the lake. The view wasn't that different from what I saw outside my dorm window, but it was just so much lovelier here. Maybe because I could see green grass instead of a cement sidewalk that led to the sandy shore. I could see branches swaying in the breeze.

I don't know how long I stood there staring out, but the timer was suddenly going off.

"Can you get the dish out of the oven?" Jordan asked.

"Sure." I set the bowl aside, slipped on the oven mitts, opened the oven door, reached in—

"Something smells good," Parker suddenly said.

I jerked up, caught my arm on the oven right above where the mitt ended—

"Ouch!"

I jumped back. Arms were suddenly around

me, hauling me toward the sink. I could smell sweat and oil and grease. Parker turned on the cold water and put my arm beneath it.

"I'm so sorry," he said. "Jordan, get some ice."

"It's not bad," I said. "Just stings."

"Still, shouldn't have happened."

He was looking at me with those green, green eyes. So apologetic, so much concern. Had anyone ever looked at me like that?

I was sure Nick would if I ever burned myself in front of him. And I might have if I'd worked in the restaurant with him. But since I'd never hurt myself, I'd never had him look as though he'd take the pain on himself if he could.

"Parker, you probably shouldn't be touching her. You're filthy," Jordan said.

He stepped back, but I could tell that he was reluctant to do it. Jordan moved into place, turned off the water, gently patted my arm dry, and looked at the burn. "That's not too bad."

It really wasn't. Maybe an inch long, a half an inch wide. I'd been really lucky. The mitt had saved me from the worst of it. Jordan smoothed some aloe cream on the burn, then placed the bag of ice against my arm. I held it in place. It was going to be all right.

She spun around and faced Parker. "The way you were acting I thought we were going to have to take her to the ER."

"I felt responsible."

"You don't usually overreact."

"Guilt, okay? Let it go."

"Aren't we snappish?"

"I spent my day off working on your stupid car, and you haven't thanked me once."

"You stink. Go take a shower."

"No, I want a hug."

She started moving around the island. "No way. You're sweaty and so dirty."

Grinning broadly, he pulled off his T-shirt. He was sweaty, but he was also very trim, very fit. Wow.

"Don't you dare," she warned. "Don't you dare—"

He went after her. She screeched and headed out of the kitchen. He followed.

I heard her scream. I walked to the doorway. He'd caught her and was hugging her. She broke away.

"You are disgusting," she said. "Go shower. But hurry, everything is almost ready."

He was heading to his room when he looked back, saw me standing in the doorway. "Want a hug?"

I shook my head and stepped back out of sight.

No way would I ever admit that yeah . . . I thought maybe I did want a hug.

Chapter 11

While Parker was taking his shower, Jordan and I began setting up dinner on the counter.

"We're just going to serve it buffet style," she said. "Everyone can fill their plates and join us on the back porch."

"Something sure smells good," a girl said, standing in the doorway. "What's the special occasion?"

She had red hair, pulled back into a ponytail.

"Parker had to fix my car so I'm paying him back." Jordan jerked her thumb toward me. "This is my roomie, Megan."

"Hey, Megan. I'm Ronda."

"She's Cole's girlfriend."

"Allegedly," she said smiling.

"You've been with him, since what? Middle school?" Jordan said.

Ronda smiled. "Pretty much."

"Grab Cole and get your plates ready. Food is getting cold."

The four of us were sitting at the wicker table on the back porch when Parker joined us. He pulled over a chair and set it between Jordan and me. "How's the arm?" he asked, as he set his plate on the table.

"Fine," I said. I wasn't certain I could say the same thing about my appetite now that he was sitting beside me. His hair was still damp, and I could actually see a couple of drops of water on his eyelashes.

Why are you looking that closely? I chastised myself.

"What happened to her arm?" Ronda asked.

"She burned it taking the casserole dish out of the oven. Parker has been totally overreacting," Jordan said.

"I have not. I'm showing a little concern."

"Whatever." She perked up and smiled. "Hey, Ross."

"Hey, babe."

I looked toward the doorway and there was Ross from the first night, holding a plate full of food. He walked over and set the plate on the other side of Jordan. Then he pulled a chair to the table and sat. He leaned over and gave Jordan a quick kiss.

I cast a furtive glance at Parker, wondering how he might take the show of affection, but he didn't seem at all bothered.

"So, Jordan's car had problems?" Ross asked.

Parker nodded. "Yep. It was a mess under that hood. I can't believe I spent my day off working on it."

Jordan leaned toward him, her nose wrinkled. "That's what brothers are for."

"He's your *brother*?" I asked, before I could stop myself.

Everyone looked at me like I'd just asked the stupidest question in the whole world.

"Well, yeah. Who did you think he was?" Jordan asked.

"He never said his last name, and you seemed to really like him, and you"—I swallowed—"you were over here a lot."

"Omigod! I slept over here and you thought . . . ew!" She shuddered. "He was so not in the bed with me. Omigod!" she said again. "Ross is my boyfriend, totally, absolutely. Who did you think Ross was?"

I felt like such an idiot. "I thought you had two boyfriends?" It sounded stupid even as I gave voice to my assumptions.

"So, what? You, like, thought I was a slut?" She laughed. "Omigod. This is too much."

Parker didn't say anything at all. Just studied me, like he was slowly figuring something out. Then as though he'd figured it all out, he turned to Jordan. "Common misconception. We don't look alike."

"Thank God." Jordan laughed again. "This is really too much."

She was shaking her head, grinning.

"So, Megan, what's your position at the park?" Ronda asked, as though trying to shift the subject away from my stupidity.

"Gift shop."

"Not Hansel and Gretel's, I hope?"

"Yeah. Where do you work?"

"I work on the shows, putting them together.

We have one girl this year, Alisha, who is so talented."

"Omigod! That's our suitemate," Jordan said. "Is she really that good?"

"Good enough that you need to have your dad come up and watch her perform," Ronda said.

Parker leaned toward me and said quietly, "Our dad's a director."

"Of movies?" I asked stupidly.

He grinned. "Yeah."

I thought I understood now why Jordan had unlimited credit card use.

"Do you know famous people, then?" I asked.

"Other than our dad, you mean?"

"Yeah."

"Sure. Jordan and I have crashed a few of his parties. The thing about the famous, though, is that they're just regular people."

"But they're *famous*," I pointed out.

He shrugged. "I guess."

"That's the reason you're majoring in film? Are you planning to follow in your dad's footsteps?"

"I'd like to. Entertainment is my life."

"But you manage a roller coaster. I don't see how that's related."

"It's entertainment. It's fun, exciting, thrilling. It's an experience. For sixty seconds, people aren't thinking about work or worries."

"No, they're wondering if they'll survive."

"You say that like it's a bad thing," Cole said. "Don't you like roller coasters?"

Until that second, I hadn't realized that our conversation had an audience. I looked over to find everyone watching us, waiting. . . .

Why did I feel like I was at some addicts' anonymous meeting?

"I'm not a big roller coaster fan, no," I admitted.

"Why?" Cole asked, appearing truly perplexed.

I held out my hands. "It just doesn't appeal to me."

"But you told me that you rode Magnum Force," Jordan said.

I was so embarrassed. "I lied."

"Why?"

"Because I get tired of trying to explain

why I so don't get roller coasters."

"Could be acrophobia," Ronda said.

Cole looked at her.

"Fear of heights," she explained.

"It's not a phobia," I assured her, although I couldn't stand to ride in elevators that were on the outside of buildings.

"Or illyngophobia, fear of dizziness," Ronda said. "Or tachophobia, fear of speed." She grinned. "I aced my psychology course. There's probably a definite phobia for roller coasters, but I don't know what it is."

"I'm not afraid of anything. I have no phobia."

"She just has no interest in roller coasters," Parker said, unexpectedly coming to my defense. "We've already discussed it."

"When did you discuss it?" Jordan asked.

Parker shrugged. "Sometime when our paths crossed. The point being, it's not important. Different strokes, that's all, so give her a break."

"Aren't we touchy?" Jordan asked.

"I just fixed your car. I can unfix it, you know," he said.

Seeing them parrying back and forth, I

realized how totally insane it was that I'd thought they were anything except brother and sister. I could even see the similarities now . . . not in the eyes or the hair or the smiles, but in the mannerisms, the confidence. They were as different from each other as Sarah and I were, but I could detect shadows of similarities. I just had to look hard, and I'd really tried not to look hard at Parker.

But the truth was that looking at him was a pleasure.

Since Jordan and I had cooked, we got out of cleanup. Parker got out of it, too, since he'd fixed Jordan's car. While everyone went inside to get a brownie, I stayed on the porch, stand-ing at the railing, gazing out at the lake while twilight came.

"It's awesome, isn't it?" Parker said quietly from behind me.

I glanced over and he was extending a brownie on a paper towel.

"We're not too fancy here," he said, as though to apologize for the offering.

"That's fine." I took it, bit into the brownie. Like Parker, I preferred the original to any fancy variety.

He stood beside me, eating his brownie, without a paper towel.

"I'm just curious," he began. "All the cold shoulders you gave me, was that because you thought Jordan was my girlfriend?"

"Not completely. Like I said, I have a boyfriend."

He finished his brownie, hitched up a hip, and sat on the edge of the railing, looking at me. "What's he like?"

"Smart. Dependable, loyal—"

"Those are the same words I use to describe my dog."

I glowered at him.

He held up his hands. "Sorry, but look, I'm interested in you. Just trying to size up my competition."

"Read my lips. I'm not interested in you."

"You really shouldn't draw my attention to your lips."

I rolled my eyes. I couldn't really take

offense, though, because he said everything like it was a joke. And somehow, as much as I didn't want to, I found myself fighting to hold back a smile.

"Does he make you laugh?" he asked.

"What has that got to do with anything?"

"My father's advice when it came to women. He said, 'Find a woman you like being with, who views spending money the same way you do, and makes you laugh.'"

"Sounds like he's an expert."

"Totally. And you're avoiding my question."

I sighed. "Yes, he makes me laugh."

"That's good."

Thank goodness he didn't ask for examples, because at that precise moment I couldn't think of any time when Nick and I had laughed. I knew there had to have been laughter; I guess it just hadn't been memorable.

"So maybe you'll come back for the hump party," he said, with no hint of it being a question.

"Maybe."

I didn't know why I felt guilty. I'd come

here to work, but surely Nick didn't expect me to have no fun whatsoever. All work and no fun would make Megan a dull girl.

Only 47 Nick-less days to go, and counting. . . .

Chapter 12

"$\mathcal{S}$he wants Aunt Vic's holy terror to be ring bearer!"

The "she," of course, was Mom. Aunt Vic was my dad's youngest sister from my grand-dad's third marriage, and the holy terror was her three-year-old son, Vincent.

"Why?" I asked, beginning to think that Sarah was right and that Mom may have indeed gone off the deep end.

"Because he's cute."

"In photos, yeah, but he's like the Tasmanian Devil in person." Honestly, the kid worked up a gust of breeze wherever he went.

"Talk to her, will ya?"

"Me? This is your wedding. You talk to her."

"Come on, Megan, you're her favorite."

"Only because I'm not there."

It was Tuesday night and I'd just gotten off my shift. I was walking along the lighted sidewalk that stretched from the theme park to the dorm. To my right were the sand and the lake. People were still out on the beach, and I could hear people at the hotel pool as I walked by.

In my backpack was a wish-you-were-here postcard I'd picked up at H & G's today to send to Nick. The neat thing about a theme park is that it has lots of postcards, tiny gifts, and I'm-having-a-great-time-but-miss-you stuff. I'd actually bought a six-inch stuffed bear that I was going to send to Nick, too. Just a little something so he'd know I was thinking about him.

"It's your wedding, Sarah. You're about to become a wife. Shouldn't you be able to tell someone when you don't like something they're doing?"

"Are you saying I shouldn't get married?"

Although there were people around, especially other people walking back to the dorm after finishing their shifts, it seemed so quiet without all the rides going. I thought that unlike an hour ago, *now* someone would hear me if I screamed. And I was really tempted to do that.

"No, I'm not saying that. I'm just saying that you have to stand up for yourself."

"It's just that I can see him running around, dropping to the floor, kicking—"

"You're preaching to the choir here."

She growled. "This would have been so much easier if you had stayed here this summer."

For her maybe. No way would it have been easier for me.

"So what are you doing?" she asked, suddenly changing the subject.

"Walking home. I really like it here, Sarah."

"You *are* going to come home for my wedding, right?"

"I wouldn't miss it. Now go talk to Mom. Tell her it's your wedding and you don't want the little monster."

"Okay. Love ya, sis."

She hung up before I could say, "Love you back." Her timing was perfect. I'd arrived at the dorm. I really hoped it would be the same for her wedding. Perfect timing on everything.

Maybe I should call Mom and suggest that she lighten up.

I walked into the dorm and went to the elevators, saying hi to a couple of the people standing around.

On the sixth floor, Zoe was greeting us, like she did every night. "Hello, ladies, did everyone have a lovely night?"

There were a couple of groans, and one girl just rolled her eyes.

"It's only the beginning of summer, luvs. Wait until we really get busy," Zoe said. "Anyone want to pop in for a bit of chitchat?"

I had on other nights, but tonight I was just way too tired. "Later, Zoe," I said, as I walked past her.

I got to my room, inserted the key, opened the door—

The hallway light spilled into the room, chasing back the darkness.

Someone rolled off Jordan's bed, someone too tall to be Jordan. Ross, obviously. Still fully clothed, thank goodness. And the bed was made. So whatever I'd interrupted hadn't gotten to any embarrassing stage.

"You're home already," Jordan said, sitting up.

"It's after ten thirty."

"I just wasn't expecting you back so soon. Ross, was just, uh, Ross was just . . . you know."

Yeah, I knew.

"Hey, Ross," I said, to try to ease some of the tension in the room.

"Hey. Guess I need to go."

"Can I turn on the light?" I asked.

"Sure," Jordan said.

I flipped the switch. Poor Ross looked like he wished he was anywhere but where he was.

"Night, babe," he said, leaning down to give Jordan a quick kiss.

He edged past me, mumbling sorry as he went. He closed the door behind him. I locked it.

Jordan got out of bed, fluffed her hair that Ross had obviously already fluffed. Took a deep breath. Clapped her hands.

"We need a signal," she announced.

"A signal?" I walked to my bed and dropped my backpack on it.

"Yeah, you know, like, so we avoid embarrassing situations."

"I wasn't embarrassed." I sat on my bed and looked at her.

"It could have gotten embarrassing. I mean, Ross and me, we've been going together for two years now." She sat on the bed, folded her legs beneath her. "So sometimes, we get into some pretty heavy stuff. And okay"—she held up her hands—"part of the reason we both came here to work was so we could have a little alone time, because my dad would totally freak if he ever caught Ross in my room. You know how it is?"

"Not really. Nick and I have only been dating for three months. We're not into heavy stuff yet."

"That's cool. I'm all about not rushing into something before you're ready. But Ross, he's my one and only. My dad just doesn't get it. He keeps saying that he does get it, because he was young once, too, but that was, like, a hundred years ago. It is so not the same."

"It sounds like you're close to your dad, though."

"Oh, yeah. He's just unreasonable. What about your dad?"

"Totally cool. He was the one who suggested I work here this summer."

She gave me this look like I was really clueless. "He wanted to get you away from your boyfriend."

I scoffed. "No way."

"I'll bet you a day off that he had an ulterior motive, and it involved getting you away from your new boyfriend."

"Bet a day off?"

"Yeah. You work during the night, I work during the day, so sometime you'll work my shift so I have some extra time off."

"What? You just expect me to call up my dad and ask him?"

"No, just sometime when you're talking to him, let it slip into the conversation. We have all summer. I'm in no hurry for an extra day off."

"But you have to work my shift if you're wrong?"

"Certainly. I can dress up like Gretel. No problem."

"You're on." There was just no way that my dad was that underhanded or devious.

"All right." She got up, went to her dresser, and took out a silk scarf. "We'll keep this on the inside of the door, but if it's on the outside, then it means knock before you come in."

"Okay," I said.

"And if your boyfriend ever comes up here, then you can use it to signal me."

"I don't think Nick has any plans to come up here."

"I don't see how he can stay away. I mean, if he really loves you."

"But isn't the opposite true? If I love him, I shouldn't be able to stay here?"

"Nah. The burden of proving love is always on the guy."

So why was I the one sending teddy bears?

A thunderstorm struck late Wednesday afternoon. Which, as they'd explained in our orientation was usually bad news because all the rides had to shut down. And where do people go when the rides shut down and they want to avoid the rain?

Into the gift shops.

But what made this one worse than usual

was that it struck with such ferocity and so quickly that it knocked out the power. And left people stranded at the top of roller coasters for a couple of hours before power could be restored.

It was the main topic of conversation at the hump party. I'd decided to go because I couldn't think of a good reason not to, especially since the park closed down early, due to the weather. It just didn't seem like the rain was going to let up. Even though we got our power back, an amusement park without rides isn't very amusing.

Of course, since it was still raining, our options for where to hang out at Parker's was limited. I'd decided on the back porch. So had a lot of other people, including Parker.

Although he wasn't standing right beside me, he was close enough that I could hear what he was saying.

"Everything just stopped," he said. "Except for the screams. It was totally weird. I've heard of this happening at other parks, but never here."

"I guess the one good thing was that they

hadn't started their descent," Ross said.

They'd just reached the apex on the tallest roller coaster in the park when the power cut off.

"We have guys who inspect the rides every morning. They're like monkeys getting to the top and we talked about trying to get the people down but, man, do you know how high that thing is?" Parker asked.

"Three hundred and fifty feet," I said. "Taller than the Statue of Liberty."

Everyone looked at me, and I felt like a total fact geek. I couldn't help it. I liked trivia.

"I'm impressed that a roller coaster phobe would know that," Parker said grinning.

I ignored his phobe comment. "And it travels at a hundred and twenty-five miles per hour."

"A total rush," Parker said.

It wasn't the speed that bothered me. It was the dips, the curves, the loops, the feeling of not being in control. Plus the initial descent was almost a complete vertical drop.

"Sure you don't want to try it sometime?" he asked.

"I'm sure." I would have totally freaked if

I'd been on it when the power went out.

He left the group and moved closer to me, pressing his shoulder against the beam that supported the eave of the porch. "So what other stats do you know?"

"Not a lot. Those just stuck with me because they were so . . . incredible. It's like there has to be a limit on how high those things can safely go, how fast . . ."

"Designers will continue to push the edge."

He was wearing a T-shirt that said, "I love it when you scream!" The words were superimposed over an image of a roller coaster.

"You really like roller coasters, don't you?" I said.

"Love 'em."

"Have you ridden the one on top of that hotel in Vegas?"

"Yep. I've been to more than twenty different theme parks. My dad's a big enthusiast, so he pretty much made sure that all our summer vacations took us close to some park or another."

"So why not work at Disneyland, closer to home?"

"The key words there are *closer to home*. Sometimes it's good to just get away, you know? So why aren't you working closer to home?"

"The wedding."

He looked like he'd just been dropped from the top of Magnum Force. "You're engaged?"

I laughed. "No, my sister is. I just wasn't sure I could survive two more months of listening to my mom and sister arguing about *the* wedding."

"So what are they arguing about?"

"What *aren't* they arguing about? Name something."

"The groom."

"Actually, that's the one thing they do agree on. It's the details of the wedding that are causing the problem. Sarah doesn't exactly go for the traditional."

"No?"

I shook my head. "Her first choice was to wear a tuxedo."

He laughed. "You're kidding?"

"Nope."

"That sounds like something Jordan would do."

"How would you feel if your bride wore a tux?" I asked.

"I think it would be a hoot as long as she didn't expect me to wear a gown." He shook his head. "Nah, I don't think I'd want her to wear a tux."

"Neither did Bobby, which is the only reason that Sarah is wearing a gown, but Mom still chalked it up as a win for herself."

"She's not actually keeping score."

"Yeah, actually they both are. It's pathetic. Then Sarah comes to me and complains about Mom, then Mom will ask my opinion, and it's so awkward, because I just want Sarah to be happy, but I want Mom to be happy, too, and I sorta understand where Mom is coming from. She and Dad got married behind a grocery store—"

"What?"

I smiled. "That's how they always tell it. They got married by a justice of the peace and his office was behind the grocery store. Apparently my grandparents sat in the jury box and watched what my grandmother refuses to call 'a ceremony.' I think Mom wants Sarah's wedding to be really special because hers wasn't."

"Can't argue with the results," he said. "They're still married, right?"

"Yeah, they are. Twenty-eight years."

"My dad is on wife number three. And every wedding has been bigger and more expensive than the one that came before. There are already signs that this last one is on a downward death spiral. Mom is on boyfriend number eight. Each one younger than the one who came before." He glanced toward the lake. "So that's the reason I'm here." He looked back at me. "I just like to be far away from the madness. Talked Jordan into coming this year. Because there's going to be fallout. It's never pretty when my parents end a relationship."

"I'm so sorry—"

"Hey, it's not your fault. It happens. The sad thing is, I think Mom and Dad still love each other. They just got so busy with careers and community and one thing and another, they had no time to remember that they loved each other. It's easier to start over than to work to make something last."

"Well, my parents have definitely worked at it. I think Sarah will be fine when it comes to the marriage. I think it's a question of surviving the wedding."

"Guess you'll go home for the wedding."

He said it like a statement, not a question, but I answered anyway. "Definitely. I'm the maid of honor."

It suddenly got very quiet beyond the house. The rain had stopped. I shivered. It was really silly of me to be standing out here in jeans and a long-sleeved shirt, because the rain had brought a definite chill to the air. Everyone else had been smart enough to wander inside where they actually had a fire going.

"Here," Parker said, shrugging out of his jacket.

Before I could protest, he'd draped it over my shoulders. It enveloped me in a cocoon of warmth. "Thanks. I guess I really should go in, but it's so nice out here."

"Feel free to come visit anytime. The beach stays a lot less crowded than the one in front of the hotel."

"Thanks for the offer, but I don't have a car—"

"You have a cell phone?"

I wrinkled my brow. "Yeah."

"Can I see it?"

"Sure, it's nothing fancy. Doesn't take pictures or anything."

I dug it out of my front pocket, handed it to him, and watched in amazement as he began punching buttons.

"What are you doing?" I asked.

He handed it back to me with a grin. "Programmed in my number. Now you can call me when you want to come over and I'll come get you. I *do* have a car and it's a lot more reliable than Jordan's."

I took my phone, shoved it back into my pocket. "I'm not going to call you. That's too much trouble for you."

I turned away, looking out on the lake.

"It's only too much trouble if I think it is," he said. "And I wouldn't."

"You might change your mind. Maybe I'll call every day," I said without looking at him.

"I wouldn't change my mind if you called every hour."

I spun around and faced him. "I can't believe you keep flirting with me."

"Why not? I'm interested, and I think you are, too."

"No way am I—"

I don't remember him moving toward me, or me moving toward him, but we were suddenly kissing. . . .

And he was skillfully revealing that all my protests were a lie.

Chapter 13

<u>Thursday Night Possibilities</u>

<u>Watch Alicia perform at the Summit
Theater</u>
<u>Pros</u>: Not have a boring night writing to Nick,
telling him how much I miss him. Be with
people, laugh, have a good time.
<u>Cons</u>: Possibility of running into Parker, who I
actually ran away from Wednesday night after he
delivered that incredible, mind-numbing, mouth-
melting kiss.

<u>Stay in my room</u>
<u>Pros</u>: Lots of time to try to remember what Nick's

kisses are like. They're hot. I know they are. Not
see Parker.
<u>*Cons*</u>: *Be alone. Lonely. Living what my mother*
assures me are the best years of my life in isola-
tion.

I was sitting on my bed, staring at the words I'd written in my decision-maker. After the park closed down at ten, there was going to be a special performance at the Summit Theater, open to all the staff, so we could enjoy the show that we normally might not be able to see because we were working during the perform-ance time.

I really wanted to go. After all, Alisha would be performing, and everyone I knew planned to be there: Patti, Zoe, Lisa, Jordan. And of course, wherever Jordan was, Ross, Cole, and Parker were sure to follow.

Which was what originally caused me to pull out my decision-maker. Parker. I so did not want to see him.

I sat there trying not to relive the humiliation of not pushing Parker away when he latched his mouth onto mine. The humiliation of actually moving closer to him. I could still smell the rain mingling with his tangy scent. I thought I would never be able to smell rain without thinking of him.

When our mouths had finally unlocked, I'd been breathless and hot and shaking and terrified. And guilty. So guilty.

I kept telling myself that it was no big deal, that it was just a kiss. But I knew that if I ever learned that Nick had kissed a girl the way that I kissed Parker, it would be so over between us. Would Nick know when he looked at me that I had kissed someone else? Would he be able to tell when he kissed me that another guy had branded his unique taste on my mouth?

I snatched up my phone and punched his speed-dial number. He answered on the second ring.

"Hey," I said, and thought I sounded guilty saying it.

"Hey, Megan." I heard him yawn. Had I woken him up? "What's wrong?"

"Nothing. I just wanted to hear your voice."

"That's cool." He yawned again.

"Did I wake you?"

"Yeah, but it's okay. I was out late last night."

"Doing what?"

Did I sound suspicious, like a jealous shrew?

"When I got off work, I went to Steak 'n Shake with some of the guys."

"Who?"

"Just guys from work. We got a lot of new summer help. I don't even know if you know them. Besides, what does it matter?"

"I just feel like I'm not part of your life right now."

"Because you're not. That was your choice."

"I don't want to fight, Nick."

"I don't either, but this is hard, Megan. I see guys with their girlfriends—"

"And I see girls with their boyfriends. Look, Nick, I don't want to get into this. I just wanted to hear your voice and know that you love me."

"'Course I do."

Not exactly a resounding endorsement.

"Can you say it?"

"I love you."

"I love you, too."

We talked a little more about nothing in particular, but I didn't feel much better than I had before I called. I stared at the pros and cons again.

There was a knock on the bathroom door and Alisha walked in. "So are you coming to watch the show tonight?"

She looked so excited, so hopeful, and maybe a little nervous as well. Tonight was a dress rehearsal. Tomorrow night would be the big opening for her. I wanted to be supportive, I really did.

Pro: Be a good suitemate.

Con: Be a jerk. Okay, be a coward.

"I wouldn't miss it," I said, giving her a smile that threatened to unhinge my jaw.

And hoping I wouldn't live to regret it.

The afternoon and night seemed to take forever, probably because I spent so much of my time looking over my shoulder. I kept expecting Parker to show up and to suggest we take up where we left off the night before.

I was sure the slow progression of hours had nothing at all to do with the million and a half people who were wandering through H & G, unfolding T-shirts to look at what was on the front—even though we had samples displayed on the walls—picking up a stuffed toy to purchase, changing their mind halfway to the cash register and putting it on the shelf with the shot glasses. (I still couldn't figure out why any kid who visited Storybook Land would want a shot glass.)

There were bells and spoons and thimbles. Little collectibles. And we rotated between the cash register and cleanup, putting everything back so it didn't look like we'd been invaded by hordes—even though we had been.

So this particular day was going exceedingly slowly. I told myself that it wasn't because I was disappointed that Parker hadn't shown up. I wasn't disappointed. I was glad.

So why did I feel so let down?

It was usually close to ten thirty when we finished in the shop, because we had to undo the damage done by customers. I was still rearranging the miniature teacups when Nancy tapped me on the shoulder.

"We'll finish up in the morning," she said. "We have a show to catch tonight. You are going, right?"

"Wouldn't miss it."

Patti and I stood outside the shop while Nancy pulled down the iron gates that kept people out. A gingerbread house with iron doors. I guess it worked, though. Maintenance crews were already sweeping and cleaning and washing things down. Whenever I felt silly in my costume, I thought things could be worse. I could be scrubbing toilets.

Patti, Nancy, and I walked together to the Summit Theater.

"Giving us a special show is almost as good as what they do for us at the end of summer," Nancy said.

"What do they do?" Patti asked.

"Right after Labor Day, we go back to winter hours, so of course a lot of the staff will be leaving. So Tuesday, when they start closing the park to the public at seven again, they use skeleton crews on the rides and the park is ours."

"I think by the end of summer, the last thing I'd want is to ride another ride," I said.

"It's the camaraderie," Nancy said. "The free food and drinks don't hurt, either."

The camaraderie. That was the nice thing

about working here. Meeting all the people, from all over the world. Although right now, it seemed like maybe most of the world was trying to file into the Summit Theater. It was crowded and I somehow lost sight of Patti and Nancy.

"Hey, roomie!"

I almost groaned. My worst nightmare realized.

I felt a tug on my arm and there was Jordan standing beside me, grinning like she'd discovered the world's largest diamond. It felt good that she was so glad to see me, but I was also extremely uncomfortable because the usual suspects were with her. Including Parker.

"You're going to sit with us, right?" she asked.

How could I say no?

"Sure."

We made our way into the theater. An usher was standing there saying, "Move all the way down, move all the way down, don't leave empty seats, move all the way down. . . ."

"Think they gave him a script?" Jordan asked beside my ear.

"I'm sure they did. Don't want to leave

anything to chance."

I finally got to the row of seats we were supposed to sit in, grateful because Jordan was behind me. But when I edged my way down the row and took a seat, I looked up to find Parker moving in to take the seat beside me. How had that happened? Jordan had been right beside me, whispering in my ear!

And now Parker was sitting next to me, in uniform, his bare knee brushing up against my bare knee. I jerked my leg away. Short skirts and cargo shorts. Dangerous combination.

I didn't want to think about the pleasant spark our touching had ignited. All around us, people were talking, mumbling, excitement mounting. I wanted to enjoy the show, but I was so aware of the guy sitting next to me, distracted by his presence.

He leaned toward me and I froze, waiting.

"You mad at me or something?" he whispered.

I turned my head and there he was, his face close enough to mine that I wouldn't have to move more than an inch to have a repeat of last night's performance.

"You know what's the matter," I said. Had I been running? Why did I sound like I couldn't catch my breath?

"I'm not sure I do."

"You kissed me," I hissed.

"You kissed back," he said, lowering his voice even more so the words were more intimate.

"Because you took me off-guard."

He grinned, he actually grinned. "So if your guard weren't up, you'd be kissing me all the time?"

"That's not what I meant. Do we have to discuss this now?"

The lights dimmed. Thank goodness. I turned my attention to the stage. Let the show get started. Give me a distraction.

"We do need to discuss it," Parker whispered, "because I haven't been able to stop thinking about it."

I slid my gaze over to him, and even in the shadows, I could feel the heat in his eyes.

There was a clash of cymbals that almost had me leaping into the row in front of me. I know my reaction was clearly evident because I heard Parker chuckling.

Then music started up, curtains were pulled back, and the show began. It was quite an elaborate production with a group of people dancing and singing.

I felt Parker's mouth brush against my ear and a shiver went down my back.

"Which one is your suitemate?"

"She's not on the stage yet."

"Tell me when she is."

Like he had to ask me and not Jordan? Give me a break. He was just looking for an excuse to get near me. I should have been angry, but instead, I was . . . flattered.

I hated to admit that, even to myself, but his attention made me feel special. I quickly told myself he was probably just looking for a summer fling.

The lights went out on the stage. Everything was black. And when a spotlight hit the stage, there was Alisha. She was dressed in a sequined gown. She looked beautiful.

I leaned over to Parker. "That's her."

"Wow. She's hot."

Was that a spark of jealousy I felt? Couldn't be.

Then Alisha began to sing. Wow indeed.

I just sat there, mesmerized.

"She's really good," Parker whispered, his voice a raspy rumble.

It was then that I realized I was still leaning against him, our shoulders touching like they'd been fused together. I told myself to move away, that I didn't need to be touching him, that I didn't *want* to be touching him.

"Yeah, she is," I said, staying exactly where I was, inhaling that scent that was him.

"Let's go somewhere after this."

I swallowed hard, shook my head. I felt like I'd felt at the top of the one roller coaster that I'd ridden with my dad. Terrified of what awaited me.

"We need to talk. There's an all night pancake house. Ten minutes away."

I shook my head again. What was the harm in talking? The harm was that it might develop into another kiss. Just having his mouth this close was more temptation than I'd ever experienced.

This was insane!

Yes, he was hot, but so was Nick. Yes, he was nice, but so was Nick. Yes, he sent shivers of anticipation through me. But so did Nick. Okay, so they weren't this strong. But they were there. Parker terrified me. Nick didn't. Nick was safe, like a carousel.

Parker was the tallest, fastest, scariest thrill ride imaginable.

"I like you, Megan," he said so low that I barely heard. "I know you don't want me to, but I do. All I want is for you to go get some coffee with me."

"I don't drink coffee after dark."

"Tea, then."

I could have sworn I heard laughter in his voice.

"Water," he continued, "lemonade, milk. Some kind of liquid. Sitting across from each other, not beside each other, where we're touching."

So he'd noticed, too, and hadn't moved aside.

Why was I not surprised?

Alisha closed out her routine. The theater went dark again. I found comfort in the darkness when I turned my head and felt, but couldn't see, my nose touching Parker's cheek. "Okay."

Chapter 14

The rest of the performances were a blurred haze, and I fought not to hyperventilate after I gave Parker my answer. When the show was over, we got up and walked out of the theater without a word.

Jordan was babbling about how talented our suitemate was, and yes, their dad really did need to come see her perform. Ross kept nudging her up against his side and planting kisses on her mouth. Maybe that was the only way he'd figured out how to stop her from talking.

"So what now?" she asked when we reached the gate of the park. "What should we all do? I'm totally pumped. Couldn't go to sleep if I had to."

"Megan and I have something to take care

of. We'll catch you later," Parker said.

I was afraid Jordan was going to ask for details. Instead she just looked at me and said, "Don't forget our signal."

I figured she was glad to know she'd have the room to herself for a while.

"I won't."

Parker and I took off in a different direction, toward the costume shop. He waited outside while I changed out of my costume — not nearly as interesting a costume as Alisha had been wearing. Part of me wanted to change slowly, hoping he'd lose patience and leave. Part of me wanted to change quickly so I could see him again, find out what he wanted to "take care of."

I settled for changing somewhere in between. Storybook Land and its fairy tales were starting to get to me — now I was thinking in terms of the Three Bears.

When I got outside, Parker was still there, leaning against a lamppost. He started walking without a word, and I fell into step beside him as we headed to the parking lot. I kept expecting him to take my hand or something, but we just walked, silence surrounding us.

But it wasn't uncomfortable. It was more like how the air feels right after lightning flashes and you're waiting for the thunder to rumble.

We got to his car and he opened the passenger door for me. Nick had never done that. Not that I expected him to. I mean, I was fully capable of opening my own door, but still, it made me feel . . . special. And I so didn't want to feel special around Parker.

I slid into his car. It smelled way too much like him. I stared straight ahead while he climbed in and started it up.

Only he didn't start it up. He just sat there. Out of the corner of my eye, I could see his arm draped over the steering wheel, the way he'd turned his body so he could look at me.

Okay, I was starting to think that my agreeing to get something to drink was a big mistake. I should probably get out of the car now, before he did turn it on and took me someplace that I might not want to be.

"Relax, Megan, I'm not going to jump your bones."

I shifted around and glared at him. "I

thought we were going to a pancake house."

He reached over and tugged on one of my braids. "Can you undo your braids first, so it doesn't look like I'm sitting there with a kid?"

"I don't see what difference it makes," I mumbled, even though I began undoing them. My compromise between fast and slow. I hadn't bothered to fix my hair. Mostly because I hadn't wanted him to think I was doing anything special for him.

When I had the strands undone, I ran my fingers through my hair, shook my head, and wondered why he was grinning like the Cheshire cat.

"I really like it loose," he said.

I thought about grabbing my clip out of my backpack, but I liked the way he was looking at me.

Bad, Megan. Don't encourage him.

"Are we going to go?" I asked. It was so wrong to be attracted to this guy. I had Nick.

"Sure." He twisted around, started the car.

I breathed a sigh of relief.

We didn't talk during the short drive to the pancake house. And we ordered more than coffee and milk. I ordered a short stack of pancakes, and Parker ordered the International, which included pancakes, Belgian waffles, and French toast, plus bacon, eggs, and hash browns. The guy had an appetite.

The waitress poured him a cup of coffee and brought my milk. After she left, Parker stretched his arm along the back of the booth, reminding me of some lithe creature that was about to pounce.

"You wanted to talk?" I said.

"Like I said, I've been thinking about that kiss —"

"Well, I've been thinking about it, too, and it shouldn't have happened."

"I agree."

With a devilish grin, he reached across and nudged my chin up so my dropped jaw closed. His words were so not what I was expecting. I was thinking he was going to say that it should happen again. I was confused, mostly because — shame on me — I sorta wanted it to.

"That's . . . that's good," I finally stammered. "So it won't happen again."

"Won't happen again." Leaning forward,

he crossed his arms on the table. "So there's no reason that we can't be friends, hang out, have some summer fun."

For some reason an old Elvis Presley song about suspicious minds that my grandmother played a lot was suddenly reverberating through my head.

"You want to be just friends?"

"Sure. Why not? We're here for the summer. I like you. I do a lot of stuff with Jordan. You're her roommate, and knowing Jordan, she'll invite you to join us. If I hook up with someone else, you'll always feel like a third wheel. If I stay unattached, then when pairing takes place, you have someone to pair with." He shrugged. "And so do I. Lot less work on my part. I'll have a partner for the summer that I don't have to impress. Just hang with. Who wants to spend the summer looking for dates?"

I furrowed my brow. "Why don't I trust you?"

He pounded his fist against his chest, over his heart. "I'm hurt. It's an earnest offer. Friends for the summer. Nothing more."

"Friends."

"Friends."

"Didn't think guys and girls could be just friends."

"Sure they can. I have lots of just friends who are girls. Kate Hudson—"

"You know Kate Hudson? *The* Kate Hudson?"

"Sure. She was in one of my dad's movies. You could have fun with me, Megan. I'm an interesting guy. Be *really* nice, and maybe I'll introduce you to Orlando Bloom."

My jaw tightened. "And what does *really nice* involve?"

He grimaced, realizing his poor choice of words.

"I didn't mean it like that. I'm not expecting anything other than friendship. Be a good friend, and maybe I'll introduce you to Orlo."

Orlo? Did he really know him that well?

"I don't get it, Parker. I mean, you hanging out with me, when I have a boyfriend, will mean that I won't be alone for the summer, but what do you get out of the deal?"

"The same thing. Not being alone for the summer. Look, Megan, it's a lot of work to try to develop a relationship, especially if you want it to go beyond friendship. With you, I wouldn't have to put forth any effort. Which works for me, because basically I'm a lazy guy."

I thought about how all Jordan's car had needed was a new battery, and he'd gone to the trouble to change her oil. Lazy? I didn't think so.

But if his offer was honest and sincere, while I had Patti and Lisa to hang around with, it would also be nice to have a guy around—especially when Jordan did ask me to join her for things. Because he was right. I would start to feel awkward, in the way.

"Okay," I said, nodding. "We can be friends."

"Great." He held out his hand. "Let's shake on it."

But when I slipped my hand into his, felt the strength and warmth of his close over mine, I couldn't help but worry that I was getting in over my head.

"So you and Parker, huh?"

I looked up from the glass shelf I was

dusting at H & G to find Nancy staring down at me.

"Excuse me?"

"I saw you and Parker sitting in his car last night in the parking lot, so I just figured you and him . . ." She wiggled her eyebrows and gave me this I-know-what-you're-up-to-and-aren't-you-a-lucky-girl grin.

"No, we're just friends."

"Yeah, right. He's totally hot. And you're 'just friends.' Give me a break."

"Seriously. That's all we are."

"If you say so."

She walked off, but her skepticism hung in the air. We *were* just friends. After we'd made our agreement last night, I'd actually relaxed and enjoyed our midnight snack. The conversation had been pleasant. He'd told me all kinds of stories about his encounters with famous people. He knew everyone, and he talked about them like they were just regular people. I guess because to him they were. I mean, some of these guys were in his "media room" watching football games, cheering the same team he did. Amazing.

And no wonder Jordan's dad had given her

a credit card. She often went shopping with the stars.

After I finished dusting, I went to my place behind the cash register. Patti was working the same shift as I was, but she'd been really quiet since I'd arrived.

"Everything okay?" I asked.

"I don't approve of summer flings," she said tartly without looking at me.

"Neither do I."

"Then why are you having one?"

"I'm not."

"We were going to sit together last night."

"I lost you in the crowd."

"I saw you sitting with Parker."

"Sitting. That's all we were doing."

"You looked pretty chummy to me."

I rolled my eyes. "You know, it's really not your business, but just for the record, we are only friends."

That seemed to become my mantra for the afternoon as one person after another dropped by during his or her break and said, "You and Parker, huh?"

The guy was Mr. Popularity, and suddenly I was his girlfriend.

By the time Parker actually stopped by to see if I wanted to take my break with him, I was fuming.

"Everyone thinks there's something going on between us," I said, as we sat at the miniature table outside the Gingerbread Man and munched on our peanut-butter cookies. "It's a regular episode of *The OC* around here."

"What difference does it make what everyone thinks? We know what's what."

"How can it not bother you that people are talking about us and not even interested in hearing the truth?"

He reached across and laid his hand over mine where it rested on the table. "Megan, I grew up with gossip and tabloids. All that matters is that *we* know the truth. I'm not going to waste energy trying to convince everyone else that we're just friends. They'll see what they want to see."

"It probably doesn't help that you're holding my hand."

He grinned. "Technically, we're not holding hands."

I couldn't help but return his smile. "It's pretty darn close."

"Close only counts in horseshoes. Isn't that what they say in Texas?"

"Yeah, something like that." I knew I should probably pull my hand back, but I didn't. I left it there because his thumb had started to stroke the back of my hand and it just felt nice. Calming. Soothing.

"Jordan, Ross, Cole, Ronda, and I are going to spend next Monday out at the lake. So, friend, are you going to come?"

I narrowed my eyes, wondering if I'd been manipulated. "Why didn't you mention this last night?"

"It just came up this morning. The guy we're renting the cabin from has a boat. He asked me to take it out, keep the engine in shape. Just gonna do some cruising."

"Sure. Why not? *Friend.*"

He laughed. It was a good laugh, a carefree laugh that made me laugh in return.

I thought it would probably start the gossiping going again. But I didn't care.

I liked being with Parker. We could keep our relationship as friends. I knew we could. Even if I felt a bit of loss when he finally moved his hand away from mine. Even if I wished our break would never end.

It was the work I was avoiding. Not the being with him that I wanted to prolong.

Or at least that's what I told myself.

Only 44, no 43 Nick-less days to go, and counting. . . .

Chapter 15

We couldn't have picked a nicer day to go out on the lake. I was wearing black shorts and my red "Too Hot to Handle" halter. Which of course made Parker grin when he saw it. That he refrained from commenting surprised and pleased me at the same time. He was wearing swim trunks and a Hawaiian-print shirt. It was unbuttoned, the front flowing back as he drove the boat across the lake. I sat in the seat beside him.

I shouldn't have been impressed. My dad had a boat. It was green. Metal. Had a motor. Held two people. He used it when he went bass fishing.

This boat was a lot bigger, a lot nicer. Cole and Ronda sat in the two seats behind us. A padded bench ran along either side of the boat behind them. Jordan and Ross were sitting there. We probably could have accommodated a few more people.

Apparently, Parker and Cole had discovered a little cove last summer when they were out exploring with the guy they were house-sitting the cabin for. So we were headed there now for a little swimming, a picnic, and just general relaxation away from the hordes of people we dealt with every day. The wind and the motor created too much noise to talk, and I couldn't explain why I was having a great time. We weren't really doing anything. Maybe it was just getting away from it all.

I didn't want to contemplate that it was being with Parker. Since we'd made our agreement to be just friends, he always came to H & G during his break—whether it was his short break or his lunch break. He was always at the park when it closed and walked me back to the dorm. And he was always asking me to come with him at dawn when he took Magnum Force for its first run of the day.

He never used the word *test*, but that's what

he was doing. Testing it to make sure that it was operating properly. If I didn't want to ride it after it was declared operational for the day, I sure didn't want to ride it *before* it was declared ready to go. He kept promising that it was safe. If it was safe, why did it need to be tested?

He looked over at me now and smiled. I loved his smile. It gave the impression that he was simply glad to find me there.

"We're almost there," he shouted, and I read the words formed by his mouth more than I heard them.

He slowed the boat as we got closer to shore. I could see the tree-lined cove. When he got near enough, he cut the engine.

"Let's go, guys," he said.

He, Cole, and Ross jumped into the water. There were ropes used for mooring the boat to a dock, but of course, there was no dock here. They used the ropes to pull the boat partially onto the shore and anchored it in the sand.

Ronda, Jordan, and I handed off all our gear to them: quilts, blankets, towels, ice chests. Then using the ladder on the side of the boat, we climbed down, dropped into water that went past our knees and waded to shore. It wasn't as cold as it had been the first night that I'd waded into it. But it wasn't Texas-warm, either.

We spread out blankets and set up the bucket of fried chicken and drinks because the guys were starving. I wanted to explore but figured that it would be better to do it on a full stomach. The place was amazing. Really secluded.

"I wonder why there aren't any houses around here," I asked once we were all settled and eating.

"I think it has to do with the ghosts," Parker said.

He was sitting beside me, his bare knee touching mine. I didn't know why, but there always seemed to be some part of him touching me: his knee, his hand, his foot. It was all very innocent, and I'd grown comfortable with it. It was just the way he was.

I swallowed the chicken I'd been chewing and looked around. "The ghosts?"

"Yeah. In the late eighteen hundreds, there was a big storm. A ship sank a mile or so from here. They say twenty-seven people drowned.

And this is where they came to rest. A little bit farther down is a lighthouse. We can go look at it after we eat."

"A shipwreck?" I asked.

"The Great Lakes are huge. There have been a lot of shipwrecks. Haven't you ever heard of the *Edmund Fitzgerald*?"

"My dad has a song about it that someone sings."

"Gordon Lightfoot. Yeah, my dad does, too. Anyway, diving expeditions are searching for the wrecked ships all the time. And huge cruise ships travel the lakes. Don't you think when you look out that it's like standing at the edge of the ocean? You can't even see the far shore."

I had thought that, the first night when I walked along the sandy beach.

"Okay, so there are shipwrecks. There has to be a more practical reason that no one lives here," I said.

"It's the ghosts," Cole said. "We saw one last summer."

"Get out!" Jordan, sitting between him and Ross, shoved his shoulder.

"Hey, watch it! You almost made me drop

my drumstick," he said.

"You so did not see a ghost," she said.

"We saw something." He pointed behind us. "Right between those trees. Then it was gone."

"You're just trying to make us more cuddly," Ronda said.

"And how do ghosts do that?" I asked.

"Get us on edge and the next thing they know, we're clinging to them, like they're He-Men or something and will protect us from all harm."

"You know, there are definite disadvantages to having a girlfriend who's studying psychology," Cole said.

"So it is the cuddle factor and not real ghosts?" Jordan asked.

Strangely, I could hear the slight apprehension in her voice, like maybe the idea of ghosts really would make her more clingy.

Cole just shrugged. I peered over at Parker. He was studying his chicken thigh like he was trying to determine what it was. Was he hoping to make me cuddle with him? Was he not looking at me because he didn't want me to see the truth in his eyes?

"I don't believe in ghosts," I said.

"You will," he said in an eerie voice. "After we go to the lighthouse, you will."

As it turned out, only he and I trekked around the cove to where the lighthouse was. I've always been fascinated by lighthouses. This one was a typical tall cylinder shape, painted white with fading red around the top.

"It's not a working lighthouse, is it?" I asked as we approached.

"Nope. Hasn't been in years."

I saw the lighthouse keeper's house. It looked ramshackle, lonely, as lonely as the lighthouse. "It's kind of sad."

"Only a girl could think a building looks sad."

I peered over at him. "That is so chauvinistic."

"But true."

"You must find something interesting about it or you wouldn't have wanted to come here," I said, fully confident that the words were true.

"Haunting," he said. "There's something haunting about it."

I rolled my eyes. "You're not going to scare me with your ghost stories."

"I'm not trying to. I don't mean haunted like with apparitions. I mean haunted like . . . lonely, abandoned . . ."

"Sad?" I offered sarcastically, anything not to let on how it always rattled me when we were thinking the same thoughts. That never happened with Nick. We could be looking at an apple and we wouldn't see it as the same shade of red. Which I'd always thought was a good thing. Isn't it better to be different, so you don't bore each other?

Parker laughed. "Okay. Maybe sad does work."

We'd reached the lighthouse. Spider webs were laced at the top corners of the door. Thank goodness no spiders were in sight. It's not that I'm a scaredy cat. I just don't like spiders, or ghosts, or roller coasters . . . okay, basically anything on *Fear Factor* is at the top of my list of things I'd rather not experience.

Parker pushed on the door. The hinges creaked. All I could see was the darkness. He took my hand. I didn't object. As a matter of fact, I squeezed his hand hard, just in case he decided to let go. No way was that going to happen.

Once we were inside, my eyes adjusted to the shadows. Faint light was spilling down from the top where there were windows, and I could see the cast-iron spiral staircase that wound its way up. Without a word, Parker started up the stairs, with me following close on his heels, not only because he was still holding my hand, but because I didn't want to be left alone.

Our footsteps echoed a clanging sound. The wind was whistling up the stairs, creating an eerie howling. Or at least I kept telling myself it was the wind. I could barely feel it, but it was there. It wasn't those souls lost to the deep making the noise and sending chills along my spine.

And I looked up constantly, not down. It was that afraid-of-heights thing that I had. The cast-iron steps were a latticework of holes. Looking down meant seeing how far up we'd gone. Better to look up and see how close we were to reaching the top.

When we did reach the top, I couldn't imagine what I was thinking. Heights weren't my thing. Yet here I was, trying not to think about how I was going to get back down.

A hollow sound echoed around us as we walked the perimeter of the room. An emptiness. That sadness again. A crack in one of the windows was probably responsible for the shrieking of the wind. In the center of the room was where the light had once burned.

"It must have been so lonely living out here," I said.

"I think it would be cool to live away from everything," Parker said.

He was still holding my hand. I still didn't object.

"You wouldn't like living alone," I said. "At the park, you know everyone and everyone knows you. You're Mr. Popularity. Popular people don't do well on their own. They need others."

"Oh, so now you're the psychology major? Explain to me someone who won't go on a tall ride, but will walk up to the top of a lighthouse."

"It's not the height so much as it is the plummeting drop."

"So if I could find a roller coaster without

the drop, you'd ride it?"

"Would it be a roller coaster without a drop?"

"Good point. Did you hear the ghosts?"

"It was the wind, coming in from the open door and through that cracked window there."

"Ah, come on, Megan, what's the fun in having a logical explanation for everything?"

"It's my practical nature."

"That practical nature is going to get you in trouble some day."

"What?"

He released my hand and walked to the lake side of the lighthouse. "Look how vast it is. Awesome."

I moved up beside him and couldn't help thinking that this was an incredible kissing place. I could see a lighthouse keeper's daughter sneaking up here with her boyfriend. I was glad that Parker and I had decided to be just friends, because this was the kind of place that made a girl think about passionate kisses. Especially when the sun started to go down.

"It really is nice to get away from the crowds," I said.

"Yeah, that's why Cole and I jumped on the chance to stay in the cabin, away from everything. The dorm is nice the first year or two because it gives you a chance to meet people, especially when you've never been away from home before. Eliminates that homesickness. But there are always people around. At the park all day. At the lake near the hotel. That's one of the reasons that I really like taking the roller coaster cars out first thing in the morning. It's like this. Quiet, peaceful. With the sun coming up." He looked over at me. "Even if you're not interested in riding, I wish you'd come to the park with me first thing in the morning sometime. It's a totally different place."

When he was looking at me like that, with those green eyes focused on me, I had a difficult time thinking. "I'm not much of a morning person."

"Neither am I. But some things are worth getting up for."

"You promise not to make me ride Magnum Force?"

"I wouldn't ever make you do anything you didn't want to do."

"You won't nag about it?"

"Nag is what my mom did before she and Dad got divorced. I simply ask."

"If you ask more than once, it's a nag."

He narrowed his eyes. "Okay. If that's what it takes to make you come with me in the morning, then I promise not to ask you to ride the roller coaster."

"You are a nag, but I'll go anyway."

"Great! You won't regret it. I'll come for you at six in the morning." Before I could protest at the ungodly time he'd suggested, he grabbed my hand. "Let's go swim."

Chapter 16

I loved Parker's enthusiasm as we walked back to the picnic site. He pointed out different birds and plants and strange cloud formations.

"Tell me that you're not this energetic in the mornings," I said, as we walked along. Not holding hands.

I really couldn't figure out a pattern as to when he would hold my hand. When he thought about it or when he didn't? Was it reflex or planned?

Having never been just friends with a guy, I was walking an uncharted path. I mean, I knew what to expect in a boyfriend/girlfriend situation. But with Parker, I hardly ever knew what to expect.

By the time we got back to the picnic area,

everyone else was already in the water. I kicked off my sandals. I was wearing my bathing suit underneath my clothes so I took off my shorts and top. Parker was already in his swim trunks so he just tossed his shirt onto the blanket.

He ran into the water, then dove in, and came up sputtering a short distance away. Which left only me on the shore.

"Come on, Megan!" he called out. "There are no sharks."

"I'm not a *total* chicken," I said, as I walked into the water.

It was pretty chilly, and I thought about how nice it would be to lie in the sun afterward and warm up.

"It's easier if you just go under," Jordan said. "You'll get used to it faster."

Only I didn't want to get used to it faster. I was perfectly fine taking my time.

I was up to my knees in the water, had just stepped forward when pain sliced through my foot. I screeched, stepped back, lost my balance, my arms windmilling . . .

I fell backward, went under . . .

I felt strong hands grabbing hold of me,

jerking me upward. I found my wet body against Parker's, skin to skin, as he held me in his arms.

"What happened?" he asked.

"I don't know. I felt something sting—"

"Omigod, she's bleeding," Jordan cried.

Parker carried me out of the water, set me on the blanket.

"Were you a lifeguard in another life?" I asked jokingly.

"Yeah, a couple of summers during high school," he said distractedly, while examining my foot.

"What do you think happened?" Ronda asked, kneeling beside Parker, looking at my foot.

"Broken glass maybe," he said. "I think it's going to need stitches."

"Stitches?" I practically shrieked. "You're kidding, right? I've never had stitches in my life."

I pulled my foot free of his hold, bent my knee, and tried to view the damage. But there was so much blood. "Oh," was the best I could manage. It looked ghastly.

Ross handed Parker a strip of shredded towel. Parker took my foot and began wrapping it.

"We need to get you to the hospital."

"It's just a little cut."

"You know you were swimming in a lake, not a pool. No chlorine to kill the germs. When was the last time you had a tetanus shot?"

When I was about two?

"I don't know."

"Come on. Everybody, pack up," he ordered. "We're going."

"Don't do that. It's not an emergency. We can go later."

"Now isn't the time to prove you're not a chicken," he said, and sounded seriously irritated.

I wasn't trying to prove anything. I just thought he was overreacting.

"Fine," I finally said. I wasn't really ready to go, but he was bigger than I was.

"See, I told you it wasn't that bad," I said, as we pulled away from the hospital emergency room.

When we'd arrived at the dock, Parker had

left the boat for the others to put away and he'd driven me to the hospital. Since Jordan had her car there, she and the gang had a way to get home, so I hadn't been concerned about them.

"I don't call a huge bandage wrapped around your foot and a tetanus shot not bad," Parker said.

The tetanus shot was a precaution since I wasn't sure exactly what I had stepped on. Could have been an old rusty can or something. I couldn't remember the last time that I'd had the shot before tonight and I didn't want to call my mom and ask her. I didn't want her worrying. And for some reason, as silly as it seemed, I was feeling guilty for being out having a great time. I didn't want Nick to know that I was doing anything other than working.

Silly, I know. I mean, I was certain that he was doing more than working. He was going to movies and having fun. I was sure of it.

"You should call in sick tomorrow," Parker added.

"I'm not sick. I'm just limping a little." The doctor had told me to stay off it for a day, but it was wrapped up pretty tight. I was sure it would be fine. "Besides, how can I call in sick if I'm planning to go with you in the morning?"

He gave a quick glance my way, a smile tugging up the corner of his mouth. "You're still gonna come with me tomorrow?"

"Just to watch."

"Before the summer is over, I'll have you screaming on a roller coaster."

"In your dreams."

It was strange. He got really quiet. It wasn't so much that he wasn't talking, but this heaviness settled in the car, like he wanted to say something, but didn't dare, and I had this crazy idea that maybe he really *was* having dreams about me. But was too embarrassed to tell me.

He pulled up in front of the dorm. "Wait there," he ordered as he got out of the car.

I rolled my eyes, but watched as he hurried around the front of the car and jerked open the car door. Then he reached inside, slid an arm beneath my knees—

"Hey, what are you doing?" I asked, even though I knew what he was doing.

"I'm going to carry you inside," he said.

My arms wound around his neck as he lifted me out of the car.

"You're overreacting again," I said. "Put me down. I can walk."

Even though I didn't really want to. Even though I sorta liked the fact that he was carrying me. It wasn't really romantic. We weren't kissing or hugging or gazing into each other's eyes. It was just fun and silly and I realized that the pain medication the doctor had given me to help me sleep through the night must have kicked in, because I was feeling kinda giddy.

Laughing, feeling special, and wondering about kissing Parker. Wondering if I could use the medication as an excuse to do what I'd thought about doing a dozen times throughout the afternoon.

He walked through the doors and I protested feebly. "Put me down."

"When we get to your room."

"Oh, that's it," I said. "You just want to tell people you've been to my room."

He grinned and wiggled his eyebrows, still walking to the elevator. I laughed.

"Megan?" A voice called out questioningly—and tartly.

I froze. Only one person I knew could sound both ways at the same time. It was a commanding voice, and I guess Parker reacted to it as well, because he spun around with me still in his arms, clinging to his neck.

And standing there, hands on her hips, brow furrowed in disgust, was my older sister.

Chapter 17

"*S*o how long have you been seeing this guy?"

Sarah and I were at a Starbucks. I knew it was a big mistake to drink coffee after dark, but I needed something to chase away the lethargy brought on by the pain meds. They weren't heavy duty or anything, just enough to make me not care too much that my sister had caught me in a guy's arms.

"We're not *seeing* each other," I answered.

She was wearing her judgmental, I-know-what-I-saw expression. I'd never been crazy about it.

"Sure looked like you were seeing each other to me," she said, and I could hear the disapproval in her voice.

"He was carrying me because he was worried about my foot."

"Geez, I guess all that giggling didn't exactly scream 'concern'!"

"You're not the boss of me."

How grown-up did that sound? Not very. But it was true.

"Does Nick know about him?"

Boy was that a low blow. It made me feel guilty when I had no reason to.

"There's nothing for him to know." I dumped three packets of sugar into my coffee. So now I would have a sugar *and* caffeine high. I'd be climbing the walls before I was done here.

Sarah laid her hand over mine before I ripped open another sugar packet. "Look, Megan, I know how it is to be away from home for the first time, with no parental control, no limits, complete freedom—"

I snatched my hand out from beneath hers. "It's not like that. Parker is my roommate's brother. We were all at the lake together. Just a big group, having fun. His carrying me meant absolutely nothing. We are *just friends*."

She stared at me, blinked her eyes. "You

really believe that," she said, like she couldn't believe I believed it.

"Because it's the truth," I stated emphatically.

She shook her head. "Maybe your truth, not his. He is definitely interested."

"He *was* interested, but he knows about my feelings for Nick. So we've agreed to be friends."

"Oh, God, Megan, tell me you aren't that naive. Guys can't be *just* friends with girls. It's biologically impossible."

"I didn't realize you'd suddenly become a biologist." She opened her mouth and I raised my hand to stop further commentary. "Let's agree to disagree on this situation. I'm more interested in what you're doing here and why you didn't tell me you were coming."

"I didn't tell you because I wanted to surprise you—which I did with resounding success."

"Okay. One question answered, one to go," I said, getting really irritated with her. "Why are you here? Don't you have a wedding to plan or something equally important to do?"

Sighing, she picked up a sugar packet and started flicking it like it was a miniature punching bag. "The planning is driving me crazy. I had to get away."

"I know Mom's been difficult—"

"Not Mom. Bobby."

"Bobby?" That wasn't good. "You mean, like you had a fight?"

"No." She shook her head. "It's like he doesn't care."

"He loves you, Sarah," I reassured her.

"I know that. It's not that he doesn't care about *me*. He doesn't care about the *wedding*. Every time I have to make a decision, I'll ask him for advice and he'll say, 'Whatever makes you happy.'"

She rolled her eyes, looking totally disgusted.

"What's wrong with that?" I asked.

"It doesn't help me make a decision. It just puts all of the burden on me. I don't know how to make him tell me what *he* wants."

Her constant hammering at the sugar packet wore it down. It tore and started sprinkling sugar over the table. She didn't seem to notice.

"So you came here to get away?" I asked, still not getting it.

"I came here to get advice."

"From me?"

She nodded.

"About handling Bobby?"

She nodded again.

I laughed. "Sarah, I've been dating for all of three months. I don't know anything about guys."

"That was obvious after I saw you with that guy tonight—"

"His name is Parker."

"—then you said you're just friends—"

My cell phone rang and I welcomed the distraction. I glanced at the display and thought about not answering. . . .

Decisions, decisions. Talk with Parker or talk with Sarah.

No brainer.

I flipped the phone open. "Hi."

"Hey, how'd it go with your sister?"

"It's still going."

"Good?"

"No."

"Bad, huh?"

"It's been better." I felt like we were talking in some sort of code, so Sarah wouldn't figure out exactly who was on the other end of the phone.

"Invite her to go with us in the morning," he said.

"She won't be interested."

"Try her and see. She looked majorly stressed. I know a great stress reliever."

"Magnum Force?" I asked. The other alternative was one of his kisses, which almost literally melted bones.

"You bet."

"Hold on." I moved the phone away from my ear and looked at Sarah. "It's Parker."

"I figured. Your short responses gave you away."

Ignoring her sarcasm, I said, "He wants to know if you want to ride one of the roller coasters with him in the morning before the park opens."

"You mean, like, by myself?"

"And with him. He has to test Magnum Force every morning."

She got this look in her eye that I didn't quite trust, but I knew her answer before she even spoke.

"Sure, why not?"

Because the ride is scary. But I held the words back.

I told Parker the good news, and he did sound like it was good news. I hung up thinking he was really a nice guy. To want to do something for my sister while she was here.

"I can probably get you a free pass for all the rides," I told her.

"We'll see. I'm not really here to have fun."

"Are you saying that being with me is a downer?" I asked teasingly.

"I'm saying that I'm beginning to think that I came here to run away from my problems, and that's not really a grown-up thing to do."

A chill was in the air the next morning as Sarah and I stood outside the entrance to the park, waiting for Parker. The morning sunlight was glinting off the lake. It was totally peaceful.

Even Sarah didn't seem quite so uptight. She'd stayed in the park hotel and we'd had breakfast together. We'd talked about safe things: movies, music, TV shows, shoes. It had actually been fun.

"So where is this guy?" she asked. "I don't get up at the crack of dawn for just anyone, you know?"

I smiled. "He'll be here."

And just like that, I saw him walking up the path. I guess Sarah did, too, because she murmured, "He is a fine specimen."

"I hadn't noticed," I lied.

"Yeah, right."

He was decked out in his park gear: cargo shorts, red polo shirt, sneakers. He did look really good. So what was new about that?

Nothing, except I was thinking about how he'd carried me yesterday and how it had felt to be held by him and how I really shouldn't be intrigued by him at all . . . but I was.

He was grinning broadly.

"Hey," he said, when he got near enough that he didn't have to shout. "So glad you decided to come today."

He walked past us and Sarah and I followed.

"So you do this every morning?" Sarah asked.

"Every morning."

The guard at the gate let us in without asking for our identification cards. He and Parker greeted each other, so I figured it was a morning ritual for them.

When I worked during the day, I would get to the park just before it opened to get my costume on, but by then it was already buzzing with activity: the various vendors setting up, the cleanup crew getting into position, the ride crews preparing the equipment for the day. It was never like it was now: almost eerily quiet.

The park had shade trees here and there. I could hear the leaves rustling in the early morning breeze. And that was about it. Maybe an occasional clank as people began gearing up for the day.

"How long are you staying?" Parker asked Sarah as we wended our way through the maze of sidewalks that led to Magnum Force.

"Only until tonight. So, do you have a girlfriend back home?" Sarah asked.

I gritted my teeth, incredibly tempted to stick my foot out and trip her, but it was still sore from yesterday. I was still limping slightly.

Parker didn't seem offended by Sarah's

interrogation. He just laughed and said, "Nope."

"I would think someone as good-looking as you would have lots of girlfriends," Sarah said.

"Sarah!" She was really going too far. "His love life is none of your business."

"It is if it involves you."

"We're *friends*," I said. I looked at Parker. "I'm really sorry. She has a problem with minding her own business."

"Doesn't bother me. I've got nothing to hide." He was wearing dark glasses, so it was hard to know exactly what he was thinking. "You gonna ride with your sister?"

I know my eyes got big. "No. I'm just here to watch."

"You sure?"

"I'm sure."

We got to Magnum Force and walked up the ramp. Parker had Sarah's undivided attention now as he explained all the stats: length of track, speed, highest point. You'd think he was responsible for building the thing the way he went on and the way she gushed over every detail. Had to be a roller coaster fanatic thing.

Not that I'd ever considered my sister a

fanatic, but she was sure acting like it now.

Since there were no people, the chains that usually forced the line to snake around the barriers weren't in place, so we were able to walk straight through to the set of cars that was waiting on the track. A guy was standing by the controls, punching a button here, a button there. When we got closer, I could read his tag: CHRIS (BELLINGHAM, WA).

He and Parker greeted each other. Parker helped Sarah climb into the first car. Then he looked back at me. "Sure you don't want to do this?"

I felt like such a wuss.

"Come on," Sarah said. "It'll be fun."

"If they're safe, why do they have to be tested?" I asked.

"So they *stay* safe," Parker said.

"Which means there's the possibility they aren't."

He tugged on my hair and grinned. "Can't argue with a phobe."

"I'm not a phobe."

His grin grew, revealing his dimples. "Whatever."

He climbed into the car beside Sarah, and for the first time in my life, I hated that I really didn't like roller coasters. Sitting that close to him would be . . . well, it would be nice. Except for the screaming and throwing up part.

They buckled up, then he pulled the bar down across them. He gave Chris a thumbs-up. Chris pushed a big blue button and the train of cars began the ascent. I moved to the edge of the platform and just watched.

I could tell that Sarah and Parker were talking. Great. What were they talking about? Not me, I hope. Gosh, don't let them be talking about me.

They got to the top and there was that one second of heart-stopping anticipation.

Then the park wasn't so quiet anymore.

It was echoing with Sarah's screams.

Chapter 18

"It was so awesome," Sarah said for, like, the hundredth time.

She slurped a strawberry freeze. We'd left Parker at Magnum Force and I'd taken her on a tour of the park, finally ending at Storybook Land. I was sorta delaying going to change into my costume to get ready for my shift.

I had nothing of interest to say to her roller coaster enthusiasm, so I kept quiet.

"I like Parker," she suddenly said.

I jerked my gaze up from my grape freeze and stared at her.

She shrugged. "It's not a big deal."

"Last night you were on my case about hanging out with him."

"That was before he made me feel better about Bobby."

I arched an eyebrow. "When did this happen?"

"When we were on the roller coaster. It's a long way to the top and he said that he thinks Bobby does care about the wedding, he's just not telling me what he wants because he really does want the wedding to be the way that I want it. At least he said that was the way he would be if he was getting married. Then he looked kinda green and said he had no plans to get married any time soon." She was smiling, wistful, looking off in the distance. "I need to get home to Bobby, wrap up these wedding plans."

"Okay."

She peered over at me. "After I see you in costume."

I groaned. "He told you about that, too, didn't he?"

"He said you're cute in costume."

"Cute?" I shook my head. "It's embarrassing."

"I promise not to laugh, but I do want to see you decked out. I'll hang around the park

today. Before you start your shift, we'll do dinner, then I'll head to the airport."

She did laugh when she saw me in braids.
At least, I think she was laughing at my hair.
She could have been laughing at the entire
outfit.

"You're adorable!" she cried out, in between
gasping for breath.

"Thanks a lot." I felt a little too old to be
adorable.

But when she hugged me good-bye to head
out to the airport and back home, I really started
to miss her: her laughter, her complaining, her
worrying about me. And her final parting words
kept haunting me:

"Watch out for Parker. He could get you
into a lot of trouble."

I was still trying to figure out how he was going
to get me into trouble when my shift ended. I
mean, he couldn't get me into trouble if I didn't
let him, right? And I had no plans to let him.

My plans changed just a little when I came
out of the costume shop and saw him leaning
against the wall, arms crossed over his chest.

He straightened when he saw me, and I really didn't like the way my whole body just seemed to smile because he was there waiting for me.

Just friends. Just friends. Just friends. We could be just friends. I was sure of it.

"Your sister get to the airport okay?" he asked.

"Far as I know." I kept walking toward the park exit.

"I like her," he said, as he walked beside me.

"I do, too," I admitted.

"You're supposed to say that she likes me, too."

I peered over at him. "She didn't say if she did or not."

He placed his hand over his heart. "I'm crushed. I thought a ride with me on Magnum Force would win her over."

He was being so melodramatically hurt that I couldn't help but laugh.

"Why was it so important to win her over?"

"I have this thing about not being liked. I want everyone to like me," he said.

"Don't let it go to your head, but I think she did like you a little."

"Yes!" He punched his fist into the air.

I laughed as I exited the park with him right on my heels. On the other side of the gate, he took my hand. It was dark, except for the occasional light along the sidewalk. I didn't figure he could see my cheeks turning red.

I thought I should jerk my hand free, but it was so totally innocent. Just holding hands. Just friends.

"Let's walk along the lake," he said.

Not waiting for me to answer, he guided us off the sidewalk and onto the sand. I didn't want to think about how romantic this would be if Nick was here, because it was romantic and Nick wasn't here and I wasn't supposed to have romantic thoughts around Parker.

Take your hand out of his. Take your hand out of his.

But my arm wasn't listening to my brain. It wasn't jerking away. It was leaving my hand snuggled warmly within his.

"You coming to the hump party tomorrow night?" he asked.

"Probably." I looked over at him. I could just make out his silhouette thanks to the distant lights and the moon. "It doesn't seem fair that you have to get to the park before it opens and you have to work until it closes."

"I don't work until it closes."

"But you're always at the park when I get off my shift."

"Not because I'm working."

I stumbled and he caught me. "Be careful with your foot," he said, and I could hear the genuine concern in his voice.

"My foot's fine," I said. "If you're not working till closing, then why are you at the park when I get off?"

We weren't holding hands anymore. We were much closer thanks to my lack of coordination and near stumble. We were facing each other, his hands on my waist.

"Why do you think, Megan?" he asked quietly.

"Because we're friends."

"Yeah, because we're friends."

"Sarah says that guys can't be just friends with girls."

"Sounds like a suspicious woman to me."

I thought he was going to pull me close. I thought he was going to kiss me. Instead he let go of me, took my hand, and started walking again.

"What's your boyfriend have to say these days?" he asked.

"Nick? Nothing really," I stammered. "Working hard. Keeping busy." *Hardly calling.* I didn't know why I was reluctant to mention the last. Maybe because it had me a little worried. Not that I was calling him every five minutes, but my plans for keeping in constant contact through some form of communication seemed to be falling by the wayside.

I had so much to keep me busy. Like walking slowly along the shoreline with Parker. If I'd rushed back to the dorm, I could have called Nick before it was too late. Or I could have even talked to him on my way to the dorm. I had my cell phone. But no way was I going to call him when Parker was here. Even if Parker promised not to say anything, I was afraid that Nick might sense —

Suddenly my cell phone was ringing, I was

screeching, and Parker was laughing. I reached into my pocket, grabbed my cell phone, flipped it open —

"Hello?"

"Hey."

Relief swept through me. "Hi, Nick. I was just talking about you."

"With who?"

We'd stopped walking, and I could feel Parker's gaze on me.

"Someone I work with. What are you doing?"

"Talking to you."

I laughed. "Where are you?"

"Driving home from work. Had a really bad night."

"I'm sorry," I said, like my being there would have prevented it when I knew it wouldn't. Out of the corner of my eye, I watched Parker walk to the water's edge. To give me privacy? Or because he wanted to get away from me while I was talking with my boyfriend?

" —a total pain in the butt."

I realized that I'd been distracted and hadn't been listening to Nick.

"I'm sorry. Who's a pain in the butt?"

"Tess. The new waitress I'm training."

Oh, yeah, he'd mentioned her before.

"Haven't you been listening to anything I said?" he asked.

"Yeah, but I'm really tired. Sarah showed up unexpectedly last night and we stayed up really late talking, then we got up early this morning . . . it's just been a long day. Why is Tess a pain in the butt?"

"She thinks she knows everything."

"Does she? Know everything I mean?"

"'Course not. You probably have to be here to really appreciate how hard it is to train someone who doesn't listen to what you say."

"Nick, I know you're upset that I'm not there—"

"No, Megan, I didn't mean it like that. I just meant it's hard to describe what a pain she is. You just have to see it."

"You can show me when I come home in"— oh, gosh, how many days was it?—"for the wedding," I finished, a little rattled that I couldn't remember the exact number of days I had left until I saw him. Knowing Nick, he'd pick up on it right away and it would hurt his feelings if I tried to fake it.

"God, I hope I've finished training her in thirty-nine days. She really bugs me."

Thirty-nine days. Whew. I'd thought it was forty-one.

"I'm sure you're a good trainer," I said, thinking how lonely Parker looked standing where he was.

"—you think? Cool idea?"

I grimaced. I'd stopped listening again. Was he still talking about the waitress or had he moved onto another topic?

"Totally cool," I said, unwilling to admit that I had again lost track of the conversation.

"So when do you want to do it?"

I dropped to the sand and buried my face in my free hand. "I'm sorry, Nick. What is it that we're doing?"

I heard him sigh on the other end. "Never mind."

"Come on. I'm really sorry. So tell me again."

"I was saying that we could both watch the same TV show at the same time and it would be like we were together."

"Oh, that would be nice, but I'm working nights most of this week. Guess we could watch a soap during the day."

He groaned. "No way."

I sat there wishing Nick was with me. Wishing he could hold me. Maybe Parker wasn't the only one who was lonely. "Do you miss me, Nick?" I suddenly asked.

"'Course I do. Do you miss me?"

"A lot."

Then there was the silence again.

"Guess I'd better go," Nick finally said.

"Yeah, me, too."

"Dream about me, okay?" he said, making me smile.

"Okay."

I flipped my cell phone closed and just stared at it. This long-distance relationship thing was hard, harder than I'd thought it would be.

Parker crouched beside me. "Everything okay?"

"It sucks. Him, there. Me, here."

Very slowly, he tucked my hair behind my ear. "I bet."

"I don't know if it's a good thing for you

and me to be friends," I admitted.

"Why? I'm behaving."

"Yeah, but it makes me feel guilty, like I'm keeping a secret from him."

"So tell him about me."

I laughed. "Yeah, me hanging out with a guy is going to go over really well with him."

He hadn't moved his hand from when he tucked my hair back. It was comforting to have his fingers against my head, his palm against my cheek. "Nick is my first boyfriend. I don't want to screw it up."

"You're not going to screw it up."

"I wish I was that confident."

"Come on. If Jordan can have a boyfriend for a couple of years, you can, too. You're way cooler than she is."

Only I didn't feel cool at all.

"Being with Sarah today, talking to Nick"— I shook my head—"I think I'm homesick."

"I get homesick all the time."

"Do you really?"

"Sure."

His thumb started to stroke my cheek. It was really nice. Nick held me and kissed me, but he never just comforted me. Then I realized that my thoughts were unfair. If Nick were here and I was homesick, he'd stroke my cheek, too.

I pushed myself to my feet, feeling even guiltier, because I'd wanted to stay there longer, with Parker being so close. And that was wrong. Totally wrong.

"I need to get back to the dorm," I said, like he didn't know that already.

"Let's go."

He didn't take my hand. Which was good because I wasn't sure what I'd do if he did.

Only 39, 39, 39 Nick-less days to go, and counting. . . .

Chapter 19

$\mathcal{M}$y foot healed nicely, and the days settled into a routine. Work. Eat. Play.

And always, there was Parker. Stopping by the gift shop about the time I was ready to take a break. Buying me Dippin' Dots. Waiting for me at the end of my shift. Walking me back to the dorm. Talking with me. Laughing. It seemed like we never ran out of things to talk about.

Which was so not the way things were going with Nick.

Whenever Nick called or I called Nick, it was a struggle to keep the conversation going. He'd always gripe about Tess. I'd listen, but I didn't really care. I didn't know her. He didn't care about the things going on at the park, all the rumors about all the various summer romances that had started up.

Alisha was apparently involved with the guy whose job it was to light up the stage she performed on. Lisa was hanging out with a guy who worked the Ferris wheel. Patti was seeing a guy who managed one of the lemonade stands. Everywhere I looked, I saw couples.

And so Parker and I just naturally seemed to always be together. Who else was I going to hang out with? Everyone had someone. Even Zoe the floor monitor was spotted seriously kissing a guy who worked at the House of Crazy Mirrors.

But Nick didn't want to hear about any of the summer romances. Not that I could blame him. He didn't know these people.

Which left us with very little to talk about. And that sometimes frightened me because I was afraid it would be the same when we were together again in nineteen . . . no, it was eighteen days. What would we talk about? What had we talked about before?

Homework, teachers, school, friends. What else? I racked my brain every night trying to grab on to some topic of conversation. Then it never failed. After I hung up with Nick, Parker would call. And we would talk. For more than an hour. About everything and anything: people we knew, favorite movies, actors he'd met, his family, my family. Why did I never seem to run out of topics with Parker, but I had such a hard time talking with Nick?

Those were my thoughts Tuesday night as I walked back to the dorm. Parker, of course, was walking along beside me. He was telling me about this woman he'd helped get into the first car.

"She has to be eighty, if she's a day," he said. "Uses a walker."

"Aren't there restrictions against frail people riding the roller coasters?" I asked.

"Hey, we post warnings. Ride at your own risk. She was willing to take the risk. This is the third year that I've seen her. She always comes to celebrate her birthday. This year I was ready. Gave her a 'I survived Magnum Force' T-shirt."

"That was nice of you," I said.

"Hey, gotta admire her, you know? I want to be like that when I'm old. Still searching out the thrills."

"I'll ride the carousels," I said.

"It's not an either/or option, you know. You can do both."

He was still trying to convince me to ride with him in the morning. Roller coaster fanatics seemed to have a one-track mind, which I figured made sense, since cars usually ran on one track. The thought made me smile.

"What's so funny?" he asked.

But I just shook my head. My cell phone rang. Of course, I answered.

"Hey!"

Silence.

"Hellooo? Nick?"

"I thought that was you," he said.

His tone of voice had a really strange undercurrent to it.

"What do you mean you 'thought'? You called me, so who were you expecting?"

"I'm also watching you."

My heart slammed against my ribs, while my gaze darted madly around.

"How can you be watching me?"

"I thought about Sarah surprising you with a visit and decided I'd do the same thing."

I stopped walking. "You're here?"

"Yeah. So who's the guy?"

Parker must have sensed my distress because he reached out to touch my face, but I backed up. "Where are you, Nick?"

Then Parker was looking around as well.

"Right behind you."

I spun around and watched in shock and amazement as Nick stepped out of the shadows.

"Nick, what are you doing here?" I asked into my cell phone, which I realized was totally ridiculous. He was here! Here! We didn't need a cell phone to communicate.

"I wanted to surprise you," he said, walking toward me, close enough for me to see that he wasn't happy. Not happy at all.

I closed my phone. "You did surprise me."

"Yeah, I can tell." He was glaring at Parker while people from the park, heading to the dorm, tried to figure out what was going on.

Some people tried to be discreet, but most didn't care if I knew they were trying to get the scoop. It was pretty obvious something worthy of gossip was going on.

"This is Parker," I said. "My roommate's brother."

"You work together?"

"We work at the park."

"It's no big deal," Parker said. "We were just walking the same way. Look around. Lots of people walking this way."

I stepped closer to Nick. I'd fantasized about him showing up. It was always one of those romantic moments: running over the sand, straight into each other's arms. Shouldn't I hug him or kiss him or something?

"How did you get here?" I asked.

"Drove nonstop."

"Why?"

"Because I miss you."

"Oh, Nick."

Then my arms were around his neck and I was hugging him tightly and he was hugging me. And all the doubts about us that I'd been having melted away.

This was Nick. My boyfriend who had driven nonstop to be with me.

What could be more romantic than that?

Chapter 20

$\mathcal{I}$ wanted to kiss Nick. I mean I really, really wanted to kiss him. I hadn't realized exactly how much I missed him until we were hugging. It just felt so good, so familiar, so the way it should be.

But a crowd of people were still walking to the dorm, and Parker was still standing there looking at us. I felt self-conscious and embarrassed. And relieved and happy and tired. Wound up.

I stepped out of Nick's embrace. "I can't believe you're here. I mean, I'll be home in a little over two weeks."

He shrugged. "I couldn't wait, Megan, but I can only stay a couple of days. Then I have to get back to Hart's."

"Where are you staying?" I asked.

"I hadn't thought that far ahead. I need my money for gas to get me back home, so I guess I'll sleep in my car."

"You'd do that for me?" I asked, feeling guilty for not missing him more, for not being willing to drive home to see him. Of course, not having a car could have factored into that decision as well.

"You can stay at my place," Parker offered.

Alarms rang in my head. No way did I want them comparing notes. Not that there was really anything to compare. Neither did I want them sizing each other up, which was sorta what they were doing now, looking at each other the way two dogs did before one decided he could take the bone away from the other.

"Who are you again, man?" Nick finally asked.

"Her roommate's brother. Megan's like my second kid sister. Just watching out for her, like I do Jordan. I've got a house up the way with a couch you can use. If you decide you want the couch, get directions from Megan. I'll leave the door unlocked. See you around."

Just like that, Parker was walking away.

"See you, Parker. Thanks!" I called after him.

He waved a hand in the air without looking back.

"What were you thanking him for?" Nick asked.

"Offering you a place to sleep, walking me home in the dark." I shrugged. "Nothing in particular." Everything in general. "I can't believe you're actually here."

We'd been standing on the sidewalk long enough that there weren't any people around anymore. He looked like he might be embarrassed or was feeling awkward. Like maybe he just realized he was here, too.

"I missed you, Megan," he said.

"So you just got in your car—"

"Yep. And drove, after scheduling a few days off. Drove nonstop."

Territory we'd already covered, but it made me feel special and loved. We weren't long-distance anymore. We were right in front of each other. I was starting at zero Nick-less days!

I threw my arms around Nick and kissed

him. He kissed me back. It felt right. It felt good. He'd driven all the way up from Texas just to see me for a few days. How cool was that?

"Don't guess I can sleep with you," Nick said.

We were lying together on one of the lounge chairs that the hotel set out on the sandy beach for the guests.

"I have a roommate and suitemates," I explained. "I'd be okay with you sleeping in the room, but I'm not sure they would be. Plus there is the whole sneaking-you-in-without-the-floor-monitor-seeing."

Not that I thought Zoe would chase him out or anything. Guys were parading in and out on our floor all the time. But as far as I knew, none stayed the night. Besides, it would be inconsiderate toward the girls I shared the suite with. They were used to walking around in their underwear.

"I can't believe you drove all the way up here without a plan," I said, surprised that I was actually a little irritated, which made no sense at all.

He was holding me close. "All I could think about was seeing you." He squeezed me tightly. "God, I miss you."

"I miss you, too, but gosh, Nick, I'll be home in eighteen days."

"I didn't want to wait."

I snuggled against him. "I'm glad you didn't."

"Do you work tomorrow?" he asked.

"Yeah. I can get you a pass into the park."

"What fun would that be, going on all the rides alone?"

"I don't go to work until the afternoon. We could hang out together until then."

"That sucks."

I rolled my eyes. "Nick, if I'd known you were coming I might have been able to switch days off with someone."

"It wouldn't have been a surprise if you'd known, and I wanted to surprise you."

"You certainly did that. And I'm not complaining. I was just explaining that I can't change my shift at the last minute."

"I know. When I started driving I wasn't thinking of anything except seeing you."

He sounded utterly defeated.

"So where are you going to sleep tonight?"

"Guess I'll sleep at your friend's, since he made the offer."

I still didn't totally like that idea, but really there was no other alternative. The dorm had a lounge, but I didn't think the management would appreciate him bunking down on one of the couches there. Besides, he needed more than a place to sleep. He needed a shower.

"What was his name again?" he asked.

"Parker."

"Parker? And he works in a park? How lame is that?"

"Nick!" I didn't know why but it felt like he'd insulted me. I felt a strong need to defend Parker. "I like his name."

"You gotta admit it's an unusual name. How many Parkers do you know?"

"It doesn't matter. Besides, he was nice enough to offer to let you use his couch."

"Whatever. I don't like the guy, Megan."

"You don't even know him."

"But apparently you do."

I sat up. "Did you see us do *anything* suspicious?"

"You were laughing."

"Oh, what? I can only laugh when I'm with you?"

He sat up and put his arm around me. It took all my willpower not to shrug out of his embrace.

"I'm sorry, Megan. I'm tired from the drive, and I guess a little disappointed that I have to sleep on some guy's couch."

I stood. "The dorm has a curfew, so I need to get inside. Guess you can sleep here if you don't want to go to Parker's."

"No, I'll go stay at his place."

"Come on, then. I'll get a piece of paper and draw you a map. It's easy to find."

"You've been to his place?"

"Sure. They have a party there every Wednesday night. We can go tomorrow."

"Thought you had to work tomorrow."

Why did he sound suspicious again?

"A lot of people work tomorrow. The party goes on late into the night so people can go over there when they get off their shift."

He followed me into the lobby, looking around, nodding with approval, like maybe he'd expected to find me living in the slums. I went to the front desk and asked Mary (Baltimore, MD) for a piece of paper and a pencil. When I finished drawing the map, I walked back to Nick.

"So where's your room?" he asked.

"Sixth floor. If we have time, I'll show you tomorrow."

We were standing there, suddenly awkward. I thought maybe he was expecting me to cave in and invite him to my room.

"I'll walk you to the door," I said.

At the door, I offered to go outside with him. "Call me as soon as you get here tomorrow," I said.

He kissed me goodnight, and I watched him walk to the parking lot to get to his car. As I went back into the dorm, I couldn't understand why I wasn't more thrilled that he was here, why it felt like an intrusion on my space.

Maybe because I hadn't planned for his arrival. My countdown was ruined. I would be home soon anyway, so why come up?

Because he missed me, and I missed him.

So why was I sorta wishing that he wasn't here? And why did it make me so sad not to be more excited to see him?

Chapter 21

The next day was the longest day of my life. It had as many hours in it as the day that had come before, but they moved along at an excruciatingly slow pace. That morning Nick had joined me for breakfast at the dorm cafeteria. They allowed guests and the food was cheap, and since Nick was seriously short on cash, it seemed to be the ideal place to eat. Then I'd gotten him a free guest pass to the park, and we'd spent the morning just walking around, hanging out on a few of the tamer rides.

That afternoon, he'd laughed hysterically when I'd come out of the costume shop. Which had sort of hurt. I mean, I knew my costume was embarrassing, but it wasn't *that* bad.

The strangest part of the day was having

Nick join me during my breaks instead of Parker. It wasn't so much that it was odd having Nick with me as it was weird not to have Parker with me. When had I started to look so forward to spending time with Parker? Why wasn't I doing cartwheels because Nick was here?

Maybe because he was being . . . difficult. That was the word.

We were at Parker's house for the weekly party, standing on the back porch, desperately searching for conversation. Anytime someone stopped by and talked to me, I'd introduce the person to Nick and he would act totally bored. I knew it was hard to feel comfortable when you didn't know people, but at least there was music and free food and drinks and the people were nice.

"I can't believe Mr. Hart hired her," Nick said.

"Who?" I asked.

He gave me an impatient look. "Haven't you been listening? I've been talking about Tess for the past couple of minutes."

"I was listening." Sorta. "Maybe you should tell him that you don't like working with her."

"It's not that I don't like working with her. She just has this attitude problem. Thinks she knows everything."

I had a vague memory of hearing this before. Why wasn't I enthralled with our conversations lately? Why couldn't I remember anything that we talked about?

"How old is she?" I asked.

"Our age."

"Do I know her?"

"Probably not. Her family just moved to town."

"She'll go to school with us in the fall?"

"Yeah."

"Maybe she's just uncomfortable being in a new place. I can relate. It's hard not knowing anyone."

Nick looked around. "No kidding. I can't believe you know all these people."

"Not all of them. Just most of them. Even if I don't know them, we have the theme park in common. Can always find something to talk about."

"When I decided to drive up here, I thought

I'd have more time with you."

"You're with me now."

"Yeah, and a hundred other people."

"You want to go somewhere else?"

"Where would we go?"

I shrugged. "I don't know."

Why was it so uncomfortable? He was my boyfriend. Shouldn't we feel at ease, regardless of where we were or what we were doing?

"Walk down to the lake with me?" he asked.

"Sure."

The music and the din of people talking got fainter the closer we got to the lake. Surprisingly the night seemed warmer than it had since I'd arrived here. We were really heading into summer. Nick was holding my hand, and I tried to be glad that he was with me, not to feel like I had to entertain him. Usually I visited with people at the party and had a much better time.

It was so unfair to Nick for me to blame him because I was bored.

What had we always talked about?

When we got to the edge of the water, he dropped my hand and stepped away from me.

"I don't get it, Megan," he said.

I stared at his shadowy silhouette. "Get what?"

"Get what you think is so great about being here." He turned around and faced me. "Don't you miss me?"

"Of course I do, Nick. I can't believe you'd even have to ask."

"Then come back home with me."

I stared at him. "Nick, I made a commitment to work here for the summer."

"And what are they going to do if you quit? Arrest you? Be mad at you? So what? You're working in a freaking gift shop. Anybody can do that."

And anyone could wait tables. And it wasn't like Hart's was the only restaurant in town or the only place he could work.

"I like being here, Nick. I like the people I've met. They're all so different and so interesting. I've made new friends—"

"And forgotten about the old ones?"

I shook my head. We'd had a similar discussion before I'd left home. Had he really just come here to hash it all out again?

"Of course I haven't forgotten about the old ones. I know it's difficult with us being apart—"

"It's impossible! I'm alone, Megan. I've got no girlfriend to go to movies with or talk to—"

"We talk on the phone."

"Big deal. I can't kiss the phone. This long-distance relationship thing just isn't working for me, Megan. If you don't come back with me, then . . ."

His voice trailed off, like he was choking up. I wondered if tears were burning his throat like they were burning mine. "Then what?" I rasped.

"Then I want to break up. I want to be free to date other people."

"Nick, I'll be home in seventeen days, and then it's just six more weeks."

I reached for him and he stepped back. "I can't do this anymore, Megan. Wondering about what you're doing and who you're doing it with."

"What are you talking about? I'm working at a theme park—"

"And hanging around with other guys—"

"Friends! Parker is a friend. I told you that.

He even gave you his couch to sleep on. Do you think he would have done that if there was something going on between us?"

"You have to choose, Megan. Me or this stupid park."

Chapter 22

Decisions, decisions . . .

<u>Go back home with Nick</u>:
<u>Pros</u>: Nick and I stay together
<u>Cons</u>: Too late to get a summer job anywhere; no money; will miss my new summer friends; giving in to Nick's demands; no compromise (do I really want a boyfriend who says it's his way or the highway?); live at home while Mom and Sarah . . .

<u>Stay here</u>:
<u>Pros</u>: Weekly paycheck; playing on the lake with new summer friends; can get to know Parker better (Will he kiss me again if I don't have

a boyfriend? Do I want him to?)
Cons: *No complaining boyfriend.*

I didn't remember choosing. I didn't remember giving Nick an answer.

It was like I suddenly woke up and found myself alone beside the lake, with his words *We're so over* echoing around me.

Just like that. A snap of the fingers. We were no longer together.

Why had he really come? Had he really thought that I would just pack up and go?

Everything was suddenly blurry, the lake seen through a mist of tears.

"You okay?"

Parker. I swiped at the tears that I didn't even realize I was crying until that moment. "I'm fine."

"Nick said he wouldn't need my couch tonight. That he was driving back home. Like, right now. That's crazy."

"As crazy as us breaking up."

"You broke up?"

"Am I in an echo chamber?"

Parker wrapped his hand around my arm and turned me. I guess I'd missed a tear or two because he ran his thumb along my cheek. "Is that why he came here? To break up with you?" he asked.

"How the hell do I know why he came here? He gave me an ultimatum. Go home with him or break up. So I guess we broke up."

"And you're sad about that?"

Were all guys idiots?

"Have you never had a girlfriend? Have you never had anyone break up with you?"

This was a first for me, and I really didn't like it. I wrapped my arms around my stomach. I wanted to double over. "Why does my stomach hurt? Shouldn't the pain be in my chest, where my heart is?"

"You need some serious heartbreak intervention," he said.

"What?"

And even as I asked it, I thought I knew where he was going with his intervention plan. A kiss to take my mind off Nick.

Only I didn't want a kiss, not even one of the

heat-seeking kind that Parker was so good at.

"I know just the thing to make you feel better."

"Nothing is going to make me feel better."

"This will. Come on."

We started walking back to the house. Parker pulled out his cell phone and called someone. I couldn't hear what he was saying. His voice was quiet, mysterious. I didn't care.

I didn't care about anything. I was devastated. I couldn't help but wonder if my mascara had run. Would people look at me and know that I'd broken up with Nick? Would they think it was my fault, that there was something wrong with me?

Should I have gone with him? Should I have thought that he meant more to me than anything else in the world? When you loved someone, weren't you always supposed to do what made that person happy?

Did that mean that I didn't really love Nick? Had I ever loved him?

Could you fall in love then fall out of love? Did you have to be together all the time in order to stay together forever?

"I don't want to go into the house," I said, as we got nearer. "I don't want to see anyone."

Parker had finished talking with whomever he'd been talking to and put away his phone.

"We'll make a wide circle around the house," he said. "We're heading for my car. I'm going to take you somewhere."

"Where?"

"It's a surprise."

I wasn't sure that I wanted any more surprises tonight.

He took me back to Thrill Ride!

A security guard was waiting for us at the entrance. I was too numb to object when the guard opened the gate and Parker nudged me through.

"Call me when you need out," the guard said.

"Thanks, Pete."

I guess when you worked here for three summers you got to know everyone.

"What are we doing here?" I asked.

"You'll see."

"I am so not riding the roller coaster." Although I was so lethargic, I might actually be able to ride it without feeling any sort of emotion at all. I was totally numb.

"Not the roller coaster," Parker said.

The park wasn't completely dark. A lot of the lights were turned off. All the lights in the buildings and a lot of the lights that lighted the path. But the lights that identified some of the more popular rides were still on. Just the signs, beaming out their names. Just enough light to see where we were going.

I supposed I should have been excited, or at least interested, to see the park when it was closed down, but I couldn't work up any sort of enthusiasm about anything. I'd never broken up with anyone before. To use Nick's favorite term, *it sucked. Big time.*

It didn't help that the carousel came into view. My favorite ride. Nick had refused to ride it with me earlier in the day. "A kiddie ride," he'd called it.

"What are we doing here?" I asked.

Parker dangled some keys in front of my

face. "I have a master key that opens the control box for all the rides. Go get on your favorite horse."

I laughed, a strange sound when I'd thought I'd never laugh again. Or at least not so soon. "You're kidding, right? Won't you get in trouble?"

"Only if I get caught. I don't plan to get caught. And I don't think you'll snitch on me. Go on. Get on a horse."

He walked over to the control box, fiddled with some switches or something, and the bright lights on the carousel were suddenly shining. I was smiling when I stepped onto the wooden platform and climbed onto a horse. A prancer. Three of its legs were down, one lifted slightly and bent. Colorful, carved flowers adorned it.

Music began to play. The horse began to move up and the platform began to rotate.

I knew it was silly, but it made me feel good, made me happy again.

As I came around in a full circle, I saw Parker standing there. He grabbed the outside pole and leaped onto the platform. He stepped over until he was standing next to me, holding the cranking rod that moved my horse up and down.

"Carousels always seemed magical to me," I admitted.

"They are magic. The horses on this carousel were carved in the late eighteen eighties. They've been renovated. Think about how many people have smiled while riding them."

"Thank you for doing this for me," I said.

"No big deal."

Only it was a big deal. He'd known what I needed more than I'd known.

"I'm sorry Nick hurt you," he said.

I was sorry, too. Sorry that maybe I'd hurt him, too, by not being willing to choose him over the park.

"I was probably silly to think that our being apart for so long wouldn't change things for us," I said.

"People do it all the time, have long-distance relationships."

"It's harder than I thought it would be," I admitted.

"It always is, and my parents haven't set the

best example, but I've seen a lot of relationships weather the storms."

"But we barely lasted a month apart."

"His loss," he said.

But it felt like mine, too.

Chapter 23

*I*t was strange to check my e-mail and not find a daily message from Nick. Not to find any silly jokes or cartoons forwarded to me. Not to call Nick before I went to bed. To not have him call me in the morning. To dust shelves at H & G's and not pick up little things to send Nick. No postcards, no wish-you-were-heres. There was just this empty place in my life.

How could I miss him more now than I had before? Although I wasn't really certain that I was missing Nick. It was more like an absence in my life, an absence of habits, expected things. And I found myself wondering, had I ever really loved Nick, or had I just loved the idea of being in love? Of having someone to go places with, someone to e-mail, someone to text message, someone to instant message, someone to call.

It had been two days. Shouldn't I be back on track by now?

Parker had walked me to the dorm after my shift. He'd pretty much carried on a one-sided conversation, telling me funny stories about different people who'd ridden the roller coaster that afternoon while he'd worked. I'd smiled but it had been an automatic reflex, trying not to be a downer.

He asked me if I wanted to catch a midnight movie somewhere. I'd said no.

Did I want to go get something to eat?

No.

Hang out at his place?

No.

He'd walked away from me with his head bent and his hands shoved into the front pockets of his jeans. And I'd wanted to cry because I'd said no only because I wanted to say yes so badly.

I was racked with guilt. Guilt because I did want to be with him, maybe I'd always wanted to be with him, and now I was feeling guilty because I'd hurt Nick. It didn't make any sense.

I went to my room. Jordan wasn't back yet, so I just turned out the light and lay on my bed in the dark, forcing myself not to e-mail Nick. Maybe I could e-mail him as a friend.

There was a knock on the door. I ignored it. It came again. I got up, turned on the light, and opened the door.

"Rescue party!" Zoe cried.

She was standing there with Jordan, Lisa, Alisha, and a couple of other girls who lived down the hall. They were all wearing bathing suits.

"What?" I said.

"Rescue party," Zoe repeated. "Heard you broke up with your boyfriend, luv. And you're moping around. Can't have that. Get your bathing suit on. We're going to the pool."

"The pool closed at ten."

"Only to the unimportant. Come on now, nothing like a late-night dip with friends to get you right back on track."

It was crazy. Everyone filed into the room

and I had this horrible fear that they were going to watch me dress.

"Come on, Megan," Jordan said, as she pulled out a drawer of my dresser and scrounged around. She tossed me my bathing suit. "It'll be fun."

"You're all insane," I said, laughing.

But still I went into the bathroom and changed. I could hear the others giggling and talking on the other side of the door.

When I stepped back into the room, they were waiting for me. And was I ever glad. Wasn't doing things with people one of the reasons I hadn't gone back home with Nick? So it was totally stupid to be moping around about it.

"Let's go!" Zoe commanded.

We hustled out of my room and headed toward the pool. It was the pool at the hotel. We had the right to use it, although I'd always thought only during certain hours. But it sorta made sense that they would let us use it when it was closed to the tourists.

"Whose idea was this?" I asked once we were outside.

Jordan turned around and started walking backward. "Mine, of course. Can't have a sad roomie. I was starting to suffer from second-hand break-up. You know? Like second-hand smoke?"

"I got it," I said, laughing. I should have known it was Jordan's idea.

As we got nearer to the pool, I could see other people hanging around within the fenced area.

"We're not alone," Lisa said.

"Not to worry. Employee e-mail is a wondrous thing," Zoe said. "I just put the word out that we were all in need of some spirit lifting."

Zoe opened the gate and we all filed into the blue-and-white-tiled pool area. Ice chests were lined up against one side.

"Brilliant!" Zoe exclaimed. "Who brought the drinks?"

A few guys admitted they'd brought them.

"How much do we owe you?" she asked.

"We raided the concession stands," one confessed. "So let's keep that little fact to ourselves."

"We've got chips over here," Lisa said. "This is great."

And it was great. To be here with so many—

"Oh!"

I found myself being lifted into someone's arms. I threw my arms around his neck. Parker. I should have known. He was grinning, but he had a mischievous gleam in his eyes.

"You know you've been a wet blanket lately," he said.

I narrowed my eyes at him. "You wouldn't dare."

"Never dare me, Megan."

He yelled and leaped for the pool. I screamed. We hit the water. Went under. Came up sputtering.

"You idiot!" I cried. I put my hands on top of his head and pushed him under.

He grabbed my legs, lifted me up, and tossed me back.

I don't know how long we wrestled until we were both laughing so hard that we were in danger of drowning.

"Feeling better, Megan?" Jordan asked from her crouched position by the pool.

I flung my hair out of my eyes.

Parker tickled my bare stomach. "Answer her."

I splashed water at him and moved out of his way. I was feeling better, so much better. I looked at him. "You know what would make me feel really better?"

He gave me a wicked grin and nodded. "Yep."

It was incredible, but I knew that he did know what I was thinking.

At the same time, we both lunged for Jordan. She screamed as we grabbed her arms and pulled her into the pool.

She came up sputtering. "No fair!"

"All is fair in love and war," Parker said.

"This isn't war, so does that mean it's love?" she asked.

I know it sounds strange, but it was like Parker suddenly got very still, very quiet.

I don't know if he was trying to come up with a witty comeback, or what it might have been. At that moment, Ross yelled "Cannonball!" and jumped into the pool, causing a tidal wave. That seemed to be the catalyst for the party to really get underway.

More people jumped into the pool. Someone turned on music. We were far enough from the hotel that I didn't think it would disturb any of the guests, the wise people who were sleeping so they'd be rested for going to the park tomorrow.

I was standing in water up to my shoulders. Parker was watching me, studying me.

"I'm fine," I finally said.

"Good. Want something to drink?"

I shook my head. "Think I'm just going to relax here for a while. I can't believe how warm the water is."

After a while I swam across the pool, got out, and slid into the Jacuzzi. The water there was really hot, bubbling around me. I scooted over until I was sitting by Jordan, who was sitting by Ross.

She leaned over to me. "It was really Parker's idea. The party here."

"As Zoe would say, 'brilliant.'"

"Don't tell him I told you," she said, her voice low.

"Why does he want it to be a secret?"

"He worries that you're vulnerable. That

you might think he's trying to take advantage of what you're going through right now." She shrugged. "Or maybe he's scared."

"Of what?"

"Of liking you and you not liking him."

"Did he tell you that?"

"Are you kidding? No way. But I see the way he looks at you. The way he's looked at you from the beginning. If you're not interested, just tell me, and I'll tell him. It won't be so hard coming from me."

"I don't know if I'm interested or not," I told her truthfully. "I just had one failed long-distance relationship."

"It's two months before we get to that part."

Yeah, but I'd had three months with Nick before ours went long-distance. We didn't even survive a month being apart. How could I build a strong enough relationship in two months to weather the long-distance part that would come? I didn't think I could.

So would it be better not to try?

Chapter 24

The pool party was a turning point. I stopped worrying about my relationship—or lack of one—with Nick. I started living in the present, enjoying every day that came along. Enjoying every minute of being with Parker.

We ate meals together, went to movies, hung out at his place. And there was always the Wednesday night party, gearing up for the weekend. Only at this party, this week, I was gearing up to leave. To go home on Friday for the wedding.

Parker and I were sitting on the back porch. Just sitting there, enjoying the evening. The really strange thing was that since I'd broken up with Nick—or he'd broken up with me—Parker hadn't kissed me. Hadn't even tried. He'd made no moves at all.

At first I'd thought maybe the whole attracted-to-me thing had been because I'd had a boyfriend. You know: You want most what you can't have.

And once I was available, well, where was the challenge? But if that was the case, why would he have kept hanging around with me? Was he waiting for me to make a move? To show I was interested?

How could he not know I was interested? We were practically living together. Except for the sleeping part, of course. But we were doing everything together, with each other whenever one of us had free time.

I enjoyed every minute of being with him, but I thought I wouldn't mind at all if he broke his just-friends pact with me and took our relationship to the next level.

All these thoughts were going through my mind as the party began winding down. People were coming out to the porch to say good-bye. If we followed our usual routine, Jordan and I would help clean up, then she, Ross, and I would go back to the dorm. The last ones to leave.

I didn't know if that would be the routine tonight. Jordan had been downing piña coladas. Ross, too. I had designated myself as the driver.

When it got really quiet and the only sounds we heard were the insects chirping, I yawned and stood up. "I guess I'd better start cleaning."

"I'll help," Parker said.

"It doesn't seem fair that you always help with the cleanup when you're the one who provides the place for the party," I said, as we walked into the house.

"I promised Mitch that I'd take care of the place," he said.

"That's right. Responsibility is your middle name."

"First name, actually."

I looked over at him and laughed. "You're kidding, right?"

"Yeah."

It was really, really quiet in the house. "It feels like we're totally alone here," I said.

"Can't be." He went to the front door, looked out. "Jordan's car is still here."

He walked back through the house. "This way," he said.

I followed him to his bedroom. And just like Goldilocks, Jordan was curled up on Parker's bed asleep. Well, not exactly like Goldilocks. Her boyfriend was snuggled up against her, both fully clothed on top of the covers.

"I *thought* she was hitting the drinks pretty hard," Parker said.

"Can you take me back to the dorm after I help you clean up?" I asked.

"Sure."

It didn't take us long. Paper plates and cups into the trash. There were never any leftovers. Put a few dishes into the dishwasher, wiped down the counters.

I was standing at the sink, staring out the window at the lake, having just rinsed out the dishrag, when Parker came up behind me, put his arms around my waist and rested his chin on my shoulder.

"I TiVo'd one of my dad's movies. Want to watch it with me?"

I looked back at him. "Now?"

"Sure. You can sleep late in the morning, right?"

"Yeah, but don't you have to get up early?"

"I don't need much sleep."

I shrugged, watched his head bob up with my movement. "Sure, I guess."

We went into the living room, sat on the couch. He put his arm around me, nestled me up against his side, turned on the TV, went through the TiVo menu, and selected a movie I'd never heard of.

"I've never seen this one."

"It's one of his better ones."

I watched the opening credits. "Sandra Bullock? I guess you know her, too."

"Yep."

"And she's just a normal person."

"They all are, Megan."

It was a romantic comedy. We were about fifteen minutes into the movie when Parker said, "You know, the thing about my dad's movies is that they're more entertaining when watched from a horizontal position."

I snapped my head around and looked at him. "Are you making a move on me, Parker?"

I thought he would smile, laugh. Instead he looked deadly serious.

"Yeah. Do you have a problem with it?"

Did I? I shook my head.

We laid down on the couch with me nestled against his side, my back against the couch so I could still watch the movie, but it suddenly wasn't making any sense to me. I'd lost the flow of the story, mostly because I was thinking about how nice it felt to be snuggling against Parker.

"I'll take you to the airport Friday," he said quietly, tucking my hair behind my ear, over and over, like it was attempting to escape from the place where he'd put it. It felt really nice.

"You'll be working. I can take the shuttle."

"I can take a couple of hours off. No problem."

"Okay. Thanks."

"When do you get back Sunday?"

"Late."

"Time?"

I smiled. "Around nine."

"That's not late, Megan. I never go to bed before one."

"It'll feel late to me after the busy weekend."

"You will come back, won't you?"

"Of course. I have half the summer left to go."

"Will you see Nick while you're there?"

"I wasn't planning on it."

He was still tucking my hair behind my ear, studying me. "You ever think about getting back together with him?"

"No."

"That's good. Look, Megan, I didn't want to rush you, I didn't want to push you. I know you were hurting, but I don't want you going home without knowing exactly what's waiting here for you."

He lowered his mouth to mine. Finally, after all this time, he was kissing me again. And I was kissing him back.

Glad that we were moving beyond the just-friends stage. Glad to know that what would be waiting for me was something that I desperately wanted.

Parker . . . and his kisses.

Chapter 25

"So have you slept with Parker yet?" Sarah asked.

I was standing in front of a mirror, making sure the gown I was going to wear tomorrow fit properly, trying to see if it needed any last-minute adjustments. Her question took me totally off-guard and I wasn't exactly sure how to answer it.

Had I slept with Parker? Yes. After an incredible kissing session on his couch Wednesday night, early Thursday morning, we'd fallen asleep. So yes, technically, we'd slept together. But I knew that wasn't what Sarah was asking.

"You know, Sarah, it's really none of your business."

"You have, then."

I rolled my eyes. "No, I haven't, not like you mean."

"Are you dating him?"

"We spend a lot of time together."

"I knew he liked you," she said. "And that you liked him."

"He's not the reason I broke up with Nick." I shook my head. "Or Nick broke up with me."

"It doesn't matter, Megan. I just want you to be happy, and you seemed really happy whenever you were around Parker."

"I do like him, Sarah. I like him a lot. It's just so natural to be with him. I can't explain it, but I'm so dreading the end of summer."

"That's weeks away. Don't sweat it. It'll work itself out. Besides, we have enough to worry about this weekend. What do you think of your gown?"

Her brow was deeply furrowed, and she was nibbling the French manicure off one of her nails. I couldn't tell her the truth.

"I thought the bridesmaid's gowns were supposed to be purple —"

"That's what I thought chartreuse was. I

didn't know it was the color of puke."

"Let's call it green with a hint of yellow. Sounds better."

Although her description was pretty accurate. She'd ordered the gowns through a catalog. The gown shown had been blue, with the other colors available just listed. I couldn't believe she'd ordered what she hadn't seen. They'd arrived yesterday. No time to send them back. What had she been thinking?

"It doesn't look that bad," I said.

"I ordered purple irises for the flowers in the church. My bouquet has purple in it. Yours has purple in it."

"It's probably got green, too, right? Stems and leaves. So it'll match the gown."

Then she did the most unsettling thing. She started crying.

I knelt in front of her and put my arms around her. "Sarah, it's all right."

"It's hideous. Your gown is hideous. Everything is going wrong."

"I hear it's good luck for your wedding to go badly. It means the marriage will last."

She looked up at me. "You're just trying to

make me feel better, right?"

"Yeah." I squeezed her hand. "Honestly, the gown isn't that bad. At least I don't look like Gretel and I don't have to wear my hair in braids."

She laughed. "That's true. I just wanted everything to be perfect, and instead, I'm just ready for it to be over."

"Tomorrow will be here before you know it."

"If we survive tonight." She scrunched up her face, and I knew she was about to deliver some really bad news.

"Tonight is just the rehearsal, then the dinner, right?" I asked.

"Right, except that the groom's parents handle the dinner and they've made reservations at Hart's. And I'm pretty sure that Nick is working tonight."

I figured my face had just turned the same shade of green as my gown. "Great."

"Yeah. I'm sorry. I just found out today—"

"Don't worry about it. Nick and I go to the same school. We're going to run into each other. I can handle it."

"Are you sure?"

"Absolutely."

I was proud of myself for sounding more confident than I felt. I wasn't sure that I was ready to see Nick again. Or if he was ready to see me.

The rehearsal went smoothly, which I'd always heard was bad luck. I didn't mention that to Sarah. She was so crazy in love with Bobby. Even though they were both totally stressed. Bobby was being a good sport, pretending to care about all the little details, but I could tell he was thinking *Let's get this over with already*.

I couldn't have agreed more.

I almost bailed out on the rehearsal dinner. I was really missing Parker, wishing I'd brought him with me so I wouldn't have to face Nick alone, which was an insane thought. I wasn't alone. There were at least two dozen people joining us in the private banquet room at Hart's.

And sure enough, our waiter was Nick. A girl with short black hair and dark eyes was assisting him. It was a little awkward when he got to me. We'd always had this private joke, because I'm so predictable. At Hart's I always ordered the chicken fried steak, extra gravy. And whenever Nick waited on me, he never actually took my order.

He'd just give me a wink and say, "I know what you want." Like the moon and stars were in alignment and we knew each other so well that we always knew what the other wanted.

But the truth was that we didn't really know each other that well. And I think that was part of the reason that our relationship didn't last. Our relationship was built on forwarded e-mail jokes and . . . convenience, if I was honest with myself.

"And what would you like?" he said, formally. Like he'd never hugged me, never kissed me, never told me he loved me.

I almost said "the usual." But in the end, I told him, "Chicken fried steak, extra gravy."

"Sides?"

"Mashed potatoes and salad with the house dressing. Sweet tea."

He moved on to the next person. I wanted to grab his arm, ask how he was. Ask if he was doing okay. If we could still be friends. But twenty-four guests were watching us, plus the girl who was following him around like a puppy on a leash.

I spent a lot of time talking to the best man, Bobby's younger brother, Joe. Probably the only guy I knew who was looking forward to school starting in the fall. He'd gone skiing last winter break and fallen in love with a girl named Kate. He couldn't wait for the fall semester to start because she would be attending the same college he was.

"Don't you think it's hard keeping a long-distance relationship going?" I asked.

"It sucks big time, for sure. But we talk every day and I've gone to see her a couple of times over the summer. She's come to see me. We make it work."

"I never thought of a relationship as being *work*," I said.

He grinned. "It's a good kind of work. I don't mind it at all."

"You just said it sucks."

"Being apart sucks. But when we're together"—I thought he was actually blushing—"she's terrific. I'm crazy about her."

"She's not going to come for the wedding?"

"No, she's traveling in Europe right now with her aunt. I get a postcard every day that says, 'Wish you were here.' I wish I was there, too."

Our conversation came to an end when Bobby's dad stood up to make a toast, to welcome Sarah into their family. Sarah looked radiant. Bobby looked so proud.

I realized that tomorrow no one was going to notice that I was wearing puke green. No one was going to notice me at all. All eyes would be on Sarah. The bride.

And that was how it should be.

When we got home, although it was late, I asked Dad if I could borrow the car for a while. I drove back to Hart's Diner and parked beside Nick's old Chevy Nova. I got out of the car and sat on the hood and waited.

Waited for most of the other cars to leave. Waited for the lights in the restaurant windows to dim and for the lights outside to go out. Only the streetlights remained on, but they were enough to see by.

I spotted Nick as soon as he came out of the building. Came out of the building with the girl who had helped him serve us. I hadn't heard her name, but I knew who she was. Tess.

He hadn't seen me yet. I watched as she wrapped her arm around his waist and he slipped his arm around her. Then he leaned down and kissed her. She laughed. So did he.

I thought maybe I should have felt a prick of hurt or jealousy or anger. But I didn't. I felt glad.

He must have finally seen me, because he staggered to a stop. Tess looked at me, looked at him.

"What's up?" she asked.

I slid off the hood. "Hi, Nick."

I walked toward them. "You must be Tess."

"Yeah, so?"

Talk about an attitude.

"Nick's told me a lot about you."

"How come?"

"This is Megan," Nick said impatiently. "What do you want?"

"I'm flying back out Sunday. I just wanted to visit with you for a bit."

He scoffed. "It's a little late, Megan."

"Yeah, I can see that. If I hurt you, Nick, I'm sorry. That's all I wanted to say. I'll see you around."

I got into my car, put the key into the ignition. A knock on the window nearly had me jumping out of my skin. It was Nick. I rolled down the window.

"Tess was here. You weren't," he said defensively.

"Were you seeing her before you drove up to see me?" I asked quietly.

He looked away, and I realized that he might have been struggling with his feelings toward Tess, just like I'd struggled with mine about Parker. That he'd driven nonstop to see me not so much because he was so desperate to be with me, but because he was afraid that he might be losing the battle to resist Tess.

"Not seriously," he finally said, before looking back at me.

"It's okay, Nick. I'm happy for you."

"I miss you sometimes," he said.

"I miss you, too. But summer will be over soon and maybe we'll be friends again."

He growled. "You know guys hate the 'let's be friends' comment."

I grinned. "I know. But I don't think we'll ever be more than friends again. So you'd better hang on to Tess."

"I will."

He reached his hand into the car, to touch my cheek, I thought, but at the last second he pulled back. "See ya."

He was gone before I could say anything.

I watched him get into his car where Tess was waiting for him. I thought about how nice it was to have someone waiting for you. Maybe that was what made long-distance relationships so hard. Because even if you had someone waiting for you, he had to wait so long.

"How's it going?"

Parker's deep voice rumbled in my ear in the dark. I'd just snuggled beneath the covers when my cell phone rang.

"Other than the fact that Sarah never learned a color chart, things aren't going too badly. My gown was supposed to be some shade of purple and instead it's after-a-roller-coaster-ride green."

He laughed. "It's not too late for them to get married here. I'll even put streamers on the roller coaster for them."

"It *is* too late. We've already had the rehearsal."

I told him about the toasts during dinner and talking with Joe. He told me about the design for the next roller coaster that he'd seen. It would be built over the winter, ready for operation next year.

We talked for over an hour, about everything and nothing. Just to hear each other's voices. And when I finally closed my cell phone, it was almost like he was there with me.

Chapter 26

When the plane landed Sunday evening, I was wiped out. The weekend had been an *emotional* roller coaster: seeing Nick; a lot of hand-holding with Sarah and reassurances that everything would go smoothly; staying up late Saturday night talking with Dad, who wanted to know everything about my job at the park. And dang it, I owed Jordan a day off, because I did get my dad to confess that he'd thought I was getting too serious with Nick and some time apart would do me good. I wondered how he'd feel about Parker? This morning I'd gotten up early to visit with Mom, who was still weepy over her firstborn daughter getting married and leaving home. I guess the weekend had been hard on everyone.

I wasn't looking forward to hauling my suitcase to the Thrill Ride! shuttle, but I figured as soon as I got to the dorm, I was going to crash. Big time.

I was thinking about the luxury of crashing as I walked from the plane to the gate. Not paying much attention to my surroundings. Suddenly someone stepped in front of me. I lifted my gaze. Smiled.

Parker.

"Hey," he said.

"Hey." I am such an amazing conversationalist that I astound myself sometimes.

He dipped his head and gave me a quick kiss. A welcoming kiss. That was the thing about Parker. I loved all his kisses. No matter how quick or how long or how slow. Each one was perfect.

"How did you get through security without a ticket?" I asked.

"I've got connections." He slipped his arm around me. "You got baggage?"

Have I got baggage. What a loaded question. Nick. The weekend with my family. Too much to unload right then and there.

"Yeah." I held up my ticket with my baggage claim number. "I wasn't expecting you to pick me up."

"Why not? You're my girlfriend, right?"

I nestled my head in the curve of his shoulder. Was I his girlfriend? For how long?

We got my luggage from baggage claim, stopped for burgers, then drove out to his place. He didn't ask me if I wanted to go there, and that was fine with me. Because it was where I wanted to be.

Now we were sitting on the grass by the lake, my back to his chest, his arms around me. Watching the moonlight dancing over the lake. It was so peaceful. I thought I could stay here forever. But we didn't have forever. We only had about six more weeks and then . . .

"I saw Nick," I said quietly.

I felt him stiffen, then relax. I wondered if he felt threatened by Nick. Parker always seemed so confident, so in charge, and yet we'd both avoided actually defining our relationship. At the airport, when he called me his girlfriend, it was the first time that he'd hinted that we were more than friends, that maybe being "just friends" hadn't worked out for us after all.

"And?" he finally asked.

I turned around so I could look at him. Even though it was night, there was enough moonlight, enough stars that I could see his face.

"It was kinda sad seeing him. I mean, I thought we had something special, that what we had could survive being apart. And it didn't. It hurts that I couldn't make it work, that it didn't last."

"So you're completely over him?"

How could I explain that seeing him again had made me realize that, as much as I'd liked being with Nick, it didn't begin to compare with how much I liked being with Parker? With Parker, it didn't matter if we were talking, if we were doing anything. Simply being with him was enough. And that was scary.

Because not having Parker was going to hurt. And in less than a month and a half I wouldn't have him in my life anymore. And apparently I sucked when it came to long-distance relationships.

"I'm totally over him," I said. I could have told him that Nick had a girlfriend, that he was totally over me as well, but it wasn't really an issue. It wasn't important. The important part was that I had absolutely no interest in Nick anymore as anything other than a friend.

Parker, on the other hand . . .

He tucked my hair behind my ear, keeping his warm palm pressed against my cheek.

"I want to be more than just friends, Megan."

"Me, too." The words came out in a raspy whisper. "But I'm no good at long-distance relationships and that's what we'll have at the end of summer." I shook my head. Maybe I was presuming too much. "I mean, we'll either just have a summer fling or we'll try and take it farther and if it doesn't last—"

He pressed a finger against my lips. "Let's just worry about now."

He drew me closer and kissed me. Slowly. Provocatively. If he was working to make me forget about the future, he was succeeding, because I was thinking only about this moment in time. His lips on mine. His hands cradling my face. The way he smelled, crisp and spicy.

When he kissed me, my mind didn't want to list out the pros and cons. I wasn't thinking about making decisions. I was totally involved in the kiss.

He drew back, nipped my chin, then started kissing me again. I loved when he did that. He took kissing to a level that I'd never experienced before him. Was it totally Parker? Or was it the two of us together, the way we meshed?

When I was with him, I felt like I was part of him. Scary. I didn't want to think about what waited for us at the end of summer. Saying good-bye. Maybe forever.

He stopped kissing me and pressed his forehead against mine. "I don't want to take you back to the dorm tonight," he said, his voice the low rumble that always shimmied through me, warming me and exciting me.

"I don't want to go back to the dorm tonight," I said.

He stood up and drew me to my feet, took my hand, and started walking back to his house.

Inside it was eerily quiet. I didn't know if Cole had already gone to bed or if he wasn't home yet. Maybe he was with Ronda. It didn't really matter. All that mattered was that I was with Parker.

The sun was just starting to peer in through the window when Parker woke me with a kiss.

"Come on, lazybones, I have to get to work," he said.

I groaned, rolled over, and buried my head beneath the pillow. "I'm not a morning person," I grumbled.

He pulled the pillow off my head. "I want you to go with me."

I peered up at him through a narrowed eye. "I'm not riding it."

"Hey! Did I ask? I just want you to be with me." He combed my hair back from my face. "Come on. Morning is the best time."

The best time for sleeping, I thought, but didn't say.

"I'll even fix breakfast while you shower," he said.

How could a girl resist an offer like that?

When I walked into the kitchen after my shower, dressed in shorts and a tank, I couldn't help but laugh at the sight of the breakfast he'd fixed for me. A bowl of Raisin Bran.

Giving me a sheepish look, he grinned. I loved his grin.

After breakfast, we drove to the park. The sun was higher, but the day echoed that stillness that you feel before most of the world is up and moving about. We walked through the park, holding hands.

Parker seemed unusually quiet this morning, like he had something important on his mind.

As we got nearer to Magnum Force, he said, "Last night you were talking about what we'd do when we got to the end of the summer."

"Yeah."

"What do you see as our options?"

"Break up or stay together. I don't see us staying together, not long-distance."

"Why?"

"Because I'm no good at it."

"A relationship takes two, you know."

I looked over at him. He was watching me.

"It's hard, Parker. Not being with someone. Just having e-mail and phone calls—"

"I know it's not easy, Megan, but if you

really care for someone, you can make it work. I really care for you."

I didn't know what to say.

He led me up the steps of Magnum Force and across the platform. He called out a greeting to the guy at the controls. "Hey, Chris."

Chris just waved.

Parker let go of my hand and stepped into the first car.

He turned back to me. "Come with me, Megan."

Shaking my head, I crossed my arms over my chest. "I can't."

He held out his hand. "Trust me."

He was more serious than I'd ever seen him, his steadfast gaze boring into me.

"Trust me," he repeated.

And I knew he was talking about more than the roller coaster. He was talking about total trust, that he wouldn't hurt me, like Nick did. That things would be different for us. That he would make them different. That *we* were different.

I was scared. My stomach tightened and my

mouth got dry. I took a deep, shuddering breath.

I put my trembling hand in his and his fingers closed around mine—sure, steadfast, secure. Symbolic of what he wanted me to know. That no matter what, he wouldn't let go. Even if we were no longer touching, he'd still be holding on. He'd be there.

I wish I could say that the little tremors of dread melted away, but they didn't. I was still terrified, not looking forward to the ride. But I wanted to be with Parker, and that meant conquering my fears.

I took another deep breath, stepped into the car, and sat on the cool leather seat. He buckled us in and pulled the bar down across our laps. I cringed at the clanking sound. Wrapped my hands around the cold metal.

"Ready?" he asked.

I swallowed hard again and nodded. He gave Chris a thumbs-up.

There was another clanking sound as the lead car began pulling the others up the track. Parker put his arm around me, leaned in, and kissed my cheek.

"It's totally safe, Megan."

I looked at him. "But it's so high and so fast—"

"Don't think about it. Just be in the now."

He kissed me, distracting me so I wasn't thinking about the fact that I was traveling at a sixty-degree angle and after I reached the apex I was going to be plummeting almost straight down at a hundred and twenty-five miles an hour.

Okay, so I was thinking about it a little, but I was also thinking about Parker and the decision to trust him that I'd made without considering pros and cons. It hadn't even required my decision-maker. And maybe that said more about my relationship with Parker than anything else. That when it came to anything involving Parker, I didn't have to list out pros and cons.

The lead car stopped for only a heartbeat, but it was long enough for Parker to pull back, grin, and say, "You're gonna love it!"

Then we were speeding down the track, the wind whipping across my face. I was screaming and laughing and he was laughing. My stomach was queasy and my heart was in my throat—

It was so exciting. Thrilling!

And so totally not how I'd thought I'd spend my summer.

Me, carousel girl, on the tallest, fastest roller coaster that the park had to offer.

As we swooped up another incline, then dashed back down, I realized that I *was* loving it . . . loving Parker. Being with him was thrilling and exciting.

The ride of a lifetime.

It felt so right. Us. The two of us together.

At that moment, I knew we could last past the end of summer. That with Parker, I could make a long-distance relationship work.

That relationships were a lot like roller coasters, filled with highs and lows, terrifying split seconds, and awesome moments when you simply enjoyed the ride.

Don't worry—summer isn't over yet! Turn the page for more romance in the sun . . .

TOURIST TRAP
by EMMA HARRISON

Cassie has her whole summer planned out, and it's going to be perfect. But then a handsome summer "invader" comes to town, and all her plans start to change . . .

SUMMER IN THE CITY
by ELIZABETH CHANDLER

Jamie loves sports and she always falls for jocks—who turn out to be jerks. But this summer she'll be in a big city, with lots of sophisticated guys. And, uh oh . . . one very adorable lacrosse coach.

Tourist Trap

by EMMA HARRISON

Finally I felt all of Lola's feet hit the ground. She steadied and I was able to wipe my hand across my eyes. Through the watery blur, I saw a bobbing, helmeted head atop an ATV, circling around the center of the meadow and heading back in our direction. I leaned down on Lola's neck and patted her, whispering soothing tones into her ear. The ATV skidded to a stop a few feet away.

"What are you doing, you psycho?" I shouted. "You almost killed us!"

Normally, I'm not the yelling kind, but my adrenaline was up and my pulse was pounding in my ears. Two seconds later and Lola and I would have been maimed.

The driver ripped his helmet off and my breath caught in my throat. As angry as I was, I knew that I had never seen anyone this beautiful before in my life—at least not outside of

InStyle magazine. The driver was about my age with sharp blue eyes and brown hair, most of which was plastered to his forehead with sweat. He had a square jaw and a tiny bit of scruff on his chin and cheekbones. Usually I would have been intimidated by the way he was glaring at me, but anger was a good look for him. He wore blue jeans, a light blue T-shirt, and a black-and-red leather racing jacket that looked as if it had been through a hurricane.

"Me!?" he shouted, standing up and tossing his helmet aside. He swung his leg over his ATV and stormed over to us. "You shouldn't even be here! You're trespassing on my property."

I laughed automatically, but then my heart sank and my throat went dry. "Your property?" I asked. "You're not—"

"Jared Kent," he said, pulling his riding gloves off.

Jared Kent. An actual Kent. The Kents were actually *here*. Donna was going to flip out when she heard about—

"And yeah, this heap of dirt is my property," he added.

Ugh! My awe and excitement was cut

· 301 ·

short just like that. Clearly the Kents were actually as obnoxious as I had always imagined. Gorgeous, I'll admit—at least this guy was— but obnoxious.

"Heap of dirt?" I replied, regaining my composure. "This is the most beautiful piece of land in upstate New York!"

"Oooh! Trees and grass! I'm so impressed," Jared said, waggling his fingers. "I can get that in Central Park, thanks."

"I knew it," I said with a laugh. "I knew you people didn't deserve to have this place."

"Excuse me?" he replied, raising his eyebrows.

"You heard me. This plot has been sitting here ignored for years and then you come out of nowhere and accuse *me* of trespassing!" I said, surprised at myself. Apparently adrenaline brought out the sarcasm in me.

"Well you are, aren't you?" he shot back.

"At least I appreciate this place!" I replied, patting Lola as she stepped sideways a bit. She wasn't much for yelling.

"Well it *belongs* to me," Jared replied. "So I think my rights trump yours."

"Typical," I said sarcastically. "It's all about who owns what. It's not like Lola and I are hurting anything riding through here. You and your ATV, however, probably just ripped up tons of grass and scared away a couple dozen animals with your little joyride." He snorted a laugh, but didn't have a comeback. I was kind of on a high-and-mighty roll.

"Who the heck *are* you, anyway?" he asked.

"Who the heck are you?" I shot back without thinking.

"I already told you that," he said.

I flushed. "Oh . . . right." So much for my roll.

Jared glanced at me, then cracked up laughing. My heart pitter-pattered in my chest, and suddenly I found myself grinning uncontrollably. Our indignation had started to sound kind of absurd—to both of us, apparently. And if anger was a good look for him, laughter was ten times better.

He's a Kent, Cassie, I told myself. *An* invader. *Get a grip.*

I sighed and dismounted, dropping to the ground in front of him. He had a couple of inches on me and had the best posture I had ever seen on a guy, holding his shoulders back and his chin up. There was a small brown birthmark next to his left eye. Totally cute. I cleared my throat and looked at the ground. If I didn't watch out, I was going to be in huge trouble here. We all knew what happened the last time a local girl found a Kent boy attractive. She became the central character of gossip for the next twenty years.

"I'm Cassandra Grace. This is Lola," I said finally.

"Lola. A pleasure," he said with a quick nod at my horse. She snorted and he grinned.

"May as well tell you now that I ride through here every morning," I admitted. "You can call the police, but they're both good friends of the family, so I'm not sure you'll get anywhere."

"*Both* of them?" Jared said, pulling his chin back. "Big precinct you got up here."

"It's just a room at town hall, but it gets the job done," I said, aware that he was teasing the town already, but chose to ignore it. It was, after all, typical invader behavior. Besides, what did I care what he thought? After this conversation I was sure I would never speak to him again. Invaders didn't talk to locals unless they were buying corn from them or paying for an oil change. Not that any of us were interested in forging deeper relationships with people who paid more money for their shoes than we did for our cars.

Jared laughed and kicked at the dirt. "You have no idea how cool it is to meet you, Cassandra Grace."

"Cassie," I said. My heart had skipped a beat when he said my name. Damn it. "And why?"

"I thought this town was going to be full of old fogies and bores," he said. "But you are clearly neither of those."

"We have lots of people who don't fall into either of those categories," I shot back. "Tons."

Jared shoved his driving gloves into the back pocket of his jeans. "Care to prove it?" he challenged.

I glanced at my watch and smirked. Okay, so maybe this conversation was going to go a little further. But only because I wanted to wipe that superior smirk of his face.

"Love to," I said.

Summer in the City

by ELIZABETH CHANDLER

Jamie,
I'm signing books. Look for the pink
flamingo on The Avenue. My table
is in front of Hometown Girl.
Love, Mom

She had attached a festival map and circled her location. Before dealing with the fuss my mother always made when she first saw me, I decided to explore the place where she had chosen to live out her dream.

Some of the crowd that swarmed the closed-off blocks of Hampden's main street were dressed for heat and humidity. But there was a guy in a red, rhinestone-decorated Elvis outfit and women of all ages with huge, teased-out hair—beehives. The beehive ladies wore cat's-eye glasses, red lipstick, and stretchy print pants. Nearly all of the women and girls carried fantastic purses. They were "Baltimore Hons"— I realized, after reading a festival poster with photos from last year's Best Hon contest. My mother had said the festival celebrated working-class women and life in the 50s, a period which, apparently, had lasted a very long time in Hampden.

I bought a large sparkly clip from a booth and pulled my hair up in a loose ponytail, then purchased a bright pink boa. It was too light to make me hot and felt very girly as it drifted around my shoulders. *Maybe this was my summer to try out* really *girly,* I thought, as I worked my way down the Avenue, carefully circumventing the area where my mother would be signing books.

I was just starting to get hungry when I came upon a parked bus painted to look like a monstrous blue can of Spam. I lost my appetite when I realized people were standing around eating Spam burgers. Next to the bus, kids were bowling, rolling small balls down an alley, trying to knock over stacked cans of Spam. I felt as if I had landed on an alien planet.

But then I saw a group of great-looking guys waiting for their chance to bowl, wolfing down the disgusting burgers, laughing and joking and being loud. With them was a Baltimore Hon, a girl as tall as I—check that, a guy! I saw it by the way he wobbled on his high-heeled mules as he crumpled up his drink cup and strode toward a trash can. I watched, smiling to myself, and at that moment, he became aware of me studying him and turned to look back.

I couldn't see his eyes—his green rhinestone sunglasses hid them—but he stared at me as if *I* were the one in drag as a Baltimore Hon. My eyes dropped to his stretchy leopard-print pants, which clung to extremely muscular legs. His feet were stuffed awkwardly into pink mules with fluffy toe pieces. I started to laugh, but he didn't. He just stared at me, so long that I turned to see if someone else, like Fat Elvis, was standing behind me. There was no one.

Feeling flirty and free in this city where I knew no one and no one knew me, I smiled and waved the end of my boa. I felt giddy with girl power, as if I had cast a spell on this guy who couldn't stop staring at me. He suddenly came to his senses, turned and walked on, but his eyes—his sunglasses—strayed back to me.

"Hey, hon, watch where you're going!" one of his friends yelled, but the guy had his eyes on me. He tripped over the street curb. Trying to catch his balance, unsteady on his high heels, he staggered wildly, then sprawled across the pavement. When he sat up next to the trash can, his red beehive wig sat cockeyed on his head. He snatched up his sunglasses, shoving them back on his face as if to keep people from recognizing him. His friends howled with laughter. The guy whirled around and hurled both fluffy pink shoes at them, realizing too late that it made him look like a girl throwing a hissy fit. Now his friends roared louder and others joined in.

The guy grabbed up his boa with a fierceness that made a flurry of feathers. I pressed the back of my hand against my mouth, but I was shaking with laughter. A big satin rose had tumbled out of his wig, and when he bent over in his leopard pants to retrieve it, it wasn't a pretty sight. A second rose that had been catapulted from his wig had rolled toward me. I picked it up, but the guy was obviously avoiding further glances in my direction, and I wasn't sure what to do with it.

"Excuse me," I called softly, as if it were possible to get his attention only.

His friends grinned at me—leered may have been a more accurate word.

"Hi, hon," one of them called to me. "What's your name?"

Now I became self-conscious and was no more willing than the guy-Hon to cross the twenty-five feet between us.

"Look, your little sweetie has your rose," one of his friends told him.

Despite the guy's tan, I could see his cheeks coloring. Mine burned as well—*"little sweetie"*—what was that supposed to mean! The guys had that cocky jock look and were eyeing my extra long legs in an obvious, obnoxious way.

The Hon glanced over at me. I threw the rose at him like a strike through the heart of home plate, then hurried off in the opposite direction.

"Baby!" my mother greeted me.

"Hey, Mom."

"Everyone, this is my baby, Jamie. Isn't she beautiful?"

"*Very* beautiful," said the man sitting next to my mother at the signing table.

"Jamie, this is Viktor."

Light-haired, blue-eyed, and thirty–something, Viktor rose to shake my hand. Whoa, I thought, is this what romance publishers look like? Then I remembered: Mom called her editor Priscilla.

"It's a pleasure to meet you," Viktor said, in an accent that I thought was Swedish. He had a body perfect for modeling skimpy gym wear. Maybe he did publicity for the chick lit line, I thought—clever marketing!

"I've got a half hour more here, baby. Would you like the house key?"

"No, I'll get something to eat and hang out."

I left Mom to her fans, but when I was about thirty feet away, I turned back to look at her, trying to see her the way a stranger would. We had the same eyes, green, and the same hair, although hers, dyed now, was a paler yellow than my streaky blond. Standing just five foot five and sporting some big curves, wearing her

hair and bangs too long for a woman who was
fifty, she looked like a country western singer —
or a romance writer, I reminded myself. I
watched a woman clutching one of Mom's
books to her breast, talking animatedly. Mom
was radiant — she had found her dream.

I found a booth selling crab cakes, and carried my sandwich and iced tea to an area in
front of the festival's main stage, choosing a seat
in the last row. Up front, members of a school
band with a color guard were wiping sweat off
their faces. Hons of all ages were gathering,
some of them practicing their poses, getting
ready for the big contest. I scanned the group
for my guy-Hon, but he wasn't there.

By the time I finished the crab cake, the heat
and long drive from Michigan had caught up
with me. Feeling pleasantly sleepy, I shut my
eyes, soaking up the June sunlight, and thought
about "my" Hon. Since he obviously wasn't
enjoying his day in drag, I figured he was being
initiated into some group. I wondered what he
looked like without the wig and make-up, what
kinds of things he liked to do, what his voice
sounded like.

"You're desperate, Jamie," I told myself, "when you have romantic thoughts about a guy in high heels." Still, I tried to imagine what would make him smile and how his laughter sounded . . .

I woke up with a start, awakened by a clash of symbols during the National Anthem. Realizing that I was the only one sitting, I rose hastily to my feet. Something rolled off my lap. I picked up a pink satin rose, the one I had thrown back at my Hon. Quickly I looked around, but he was nowhere in sight.

I studied the rose, then attached it to my shirt, wrapping its wire base around my strap. The rose was old, which made it seem as if it had once been special to someone. I touched its fabric gently, lovingly. Dropping it in my lap was the most romantic thing a guy had ever done for me.